He r

from its ribbon

"I thought I asked you to wear it loose," Benedict said.

"I don't have to do what you say," Melissa said, nervously running the tip of her tongue over her lips.

His eyes narrowed and his hands reached out to feel the silky softness of her hair. He looked deeply into her eyes. "I don't know what sort of man made you like this," he rasped, "but it's time you snapped out of it. You're really quite beautiful."

For a moment Melissa wanted him to kiss her, and then was appalled at her thought. She swung away from him.

"Are you afraid of me, Melissa?" he asked.

"No!" But she was. Very much so. It was too soon. She didn't want to get involved, not with anyone, not yet—perhaps not ever.

Margaret Mayo began writing quite by chance when the engineering company she worked for wasn't very busy and she found herself with time on her hands. Today, with more than thirty romance novels to her credit, she admits that writing governs her life to a large extent. When she and her husband holiday—Cornwall is their favorite spot—Margaret always has a notebook and camera on hand and is constantly looking for fresh ideas. She lives in the countryside near Stafford, England.

Books by Margaret Mayo

HARLEQUIN ROMANCE

2280—AFRAID TO LOVE
2327—STORMY AFFAIR
2360—VALLEY OF THE HAWK
2385—BURNING DESIRE
2439—A TASTE OF PARADISE
2474—DIVIDED LOYALTIES
2557—DANGEROUS JOURNEY
2602—RETURN A STRANGER
2795—IMPULSIVE CHALLENGE
2805—AT DAGGERS DRAWN

HARLEQUIN PRESENTS

963—PASSIONATE VENGEANCE
1045—SAVAGE AFFAIR
1108—A PAINFUL LOVING

Feelings
Margaret Mayo

Harlequin Books

TORONTO • NEW YORK • LONDON
AMSTERDAM • PARIS • SYDNEY • HAMBURG
STOCKHOLM • ATHENS • TOKYO • MILAN

Original hardcover edition published in 1988
by Mills & Boon Limited

ISBN 0-373-02937-3

Harlequin Romance first edition October 1988

CHAPTER ONE

'I DON'T care. I have to get away. I can't stay here a moment longer. Can't you understand?'

Mrs Sutherland looked sadly at her daughter. 'Running away won't solve your problem.'

'But don't you see what it's doing to me?' Melissa's wide green eyes were full of pain, her face unusually pale, the skin drawn tightly over her cheekbones. 'I can't go on like this, seeing Tim every day, knowing that it's all over.'

It was like facing a death sentence. Couldn't her mother understand that?

'It was cruel of him, I know, to let you down.' Mrs Sutherland, fifty-one, greying, but with a still fine figure, smiled gently as she searched for the right words. 'But to be truthful, I'm glad he did it at this stage. He obviously doesn't love you enough for such a commitment. Two broken marriages in the family is enough; I wouldn't have liked to see a third.'

Melissa took a deep breath, letting it out slowly and resignedly. It had not been easy for her mother bringing up two daughters on her own, her father having walked out on them when Melissa was only six. And when big sister Melanie's husband had left her after only twelve months of marriage it had made Melissa wonder if any man found it possible to remain faithful. She had thanked the lord for Tim. And now he had done the same to her!

'I know you're right, Mum, but it doesn't make it any easier. I want to get away, completely away. Away from men altogether,' she added vehemently.

Her mother grimaced. 'There's not much chance of that.' Then her face lit up. 'Vivienne phoned last night. She's looking for a new secretary. How about if I put in a word for you?'

Aunt Viv? In Oxford? Perfect. The more miles between her and Tim the better. And a woman employer? What more could she ask for?

Melissa was not vain, but her thick chestnut hair and her wide vivid green eyes were a magnet where men were concerned. Only by constantly flaunting her engagement ring under their noses was she able to keep them at bay. Tim had been the only man she had wanted for as long as she could remember.

'Yes,' she said firmly at this point in her thoughts. 'It sounds a good idea. Yes, I think I'd like that.'

Her mother looked relieved; she hated seeing her daughter unhappy. 'I'll ring Vivienne now.'

A week later, thanks to her understanding and sympathetic boss—though he was disappointed to be losing such an efficient secretary—Melissa arrived at Vivienne's house.

It was a three-storeyed Edwardian building on the outskirts of the city with steps leading straight up from the street to the front door. Melissa had not been there for years, but it still looked exactly as she remembered it: black and white paintwork and a huge brass Louis XV laughing-face door-knocker.

Melissa felt apprehensive about this new job, as it was

more a personal assistant Vivienne wanted than a secretary, and she knew nothing at all about advertising. But Vivienne had assured her she could do it, so here she was, glad at least that she would not be seeing Tim at every turn.

Vivienne Winters flung open the door, her smile welcoming. 'Melly, my love. Oh, my God, you look awful!'

Honest to the point of rudeness, that was Vivienne; a tall, glamorous woman, with excellent bone structure and heavy gold hair cut in a chic gamine style. Melissa dug up a smile from somewhere, though heaven knew she didn't feel like smiling. She had not smiled in two weeks. She didn't think she ever would again. 'Thanks, Aunt Viv, you're just what I need.'

'Oh, I'm sorry, love, but honestly, you don't look the same person.' She picked up one of Melissa's cases and led the way inside. 'I wish I could get my hands on that Timothy, I'd sure like to tell him what I think of him.'

'Mum says it's for the best,' admitted Melissa, not sounding as though she believed it.

'But to jilt you on the eve of your wedding. How much more cruel could he be?' Vivienne's widely spaced brown eyes flashed angrily.

'Not to turn up at the church?' suggested Melissa.

'I've known that happen,' snorted Vivienne. 'And you've done the right thing. It's all very well loving your next-door neighbour, but I can imagine the hell once it's finished. There's no getting away, is there?'

Melissa shook her head miserably.

'Give yourself a week or two and you'll wonder what all the fuss was about.'

'It will take more than that, Aunt Viv. You're forgetting I've known Tim all my life. I feel as though I've lost my right arm.'

'Mmm.' Vivienne looked thoughtful. 'I'm wondering whether perhaps you didn't drift into a relationship that wasn't exactly right. Maybe Tim saw it before you did. Maybe you ought to be thankful—instead of upset?'

So everyone kept telling her, but Melissa could not accept it. Tim had let her down. Dear tried and tested Tim, the one man in the whole wide world she would have laid her life on as being solid and dependable. Her lip quivered and she turned away.

Vivienne smiled sympathetically. 'Come on, I'll show you to your room.'

When she had showered and changed Melissa felt slightly better. She studied her reflection in the mirror. No wonder Aunt Viv had had a shock. This was the new Melissa. Conscious of an intense desire to shut men out of her life, for a while at least, if not for ever, she had scraped back her hair into an unbecoming bun.

It did not suit her off her face; she had too high a forehead. She look most unattractive. Thank goodness. Her face was scrubbed clean, bare of make-up, and because she had not been sleeping or eating there were hollows in her cheeks and purple shadows beneath her eyes. She smiled. No man would fancy her now.

Back downstairs, eating supper, Vivienne surprised her by announcing that she had to go to New York for a few days. 'But you can always call on Beebee if you're in trouble.'

Melissa frowned. 'Who's Beebee?'

'Beebee's my partner, and lives in a self-contained flat

on the top floor,' dismissed Vivienne lightly.

'Oh, I see,' said Melissa. She had not known Vivienne had a partner, had always thought that she ran the business herself.

'Obviously I'll take you into the office and introduce you to everyone before I leave,' Vivienne went on. 'And Beebee will take over my work while I'm away. You'll have plenty to do. I'm sorry, Melly, that it's happened like this. I really am. I'd quite forgotten I'd be away.'

'Don't worry, Aunt Viv, I'll be fine,' reassured Melissa. The evenings would be the worst, giving her time to think, but it couldn't be helped. She didn't hold it against Vivienne for forgetting.

'Let's drop the "aunt", shall we?' suggested Vivienne. 'It was all right when you and Melanie were kids, but as my assistant it will hardly be right and, besides, it makes me feel old.'

Vivienne would never be old, decided Melissa. She was ageless. She was actually her mother's friend, had never married, and was a dedicated and very successful career woman. In her early fifties, she looked forty, and her face and figure were as good now as they had ever been.

Melissa slept little that night, still haunted by thoughts of Tim. Ever since the evil day she had suffered nightmares, and they were no less intense now.

She approved her own image in the mirror the next morning, her face still nude, her dress loose, hiding her voluptuous curves. Her breasts, though firm and proud, were fuller than she would have liked, and whereas Tim had preferred her to wear tight-fitting sweaters, her own choice was something concealing.

Vivienne pursed her lips when she saw her, then a smile

crept through. 'I doubt if it will keep them at bay, Melly. You're still a very attractive girl.'

In contrast Vivienne was wearing a cream, slim-fitting, woollen dress and a chunky amber necklace. Her hair was shining and immaculate, her nails long and polished. The epitome of a successful woman.

Melissa wondered whether she was being fair on her mother's friend. To be truthful, she knew she wasn't being fair to herself. She did not feel good, looking like this, but, for the time being at least, it was a necessity. Her defence against the wicked men in this world.

Vivienne's suite of offices was on the top floor of a modern office block in the centre of Oxford. As they settled the car in the basement car park, Melissa observed a fierce black Porsche swing in behind them. The windscreen was tinted and the man barely visible in the gloom of the parking area. Melissa would have liked to see who drove such a monster, but as Vivienne had strode on ahead she dared not wait to find out.

An express lift whizzed them upwards and they exited on to the soft grey carpet of the reception area. The walls were draped with pink silk, cherubs stood on pillars, plants cascaded from urns and tubs. There were no windows but the lighting was dramatic, and Melissa stood in awe.

'You approve, I hope?' smiled Vivienne.

'It's beautiful,' said Melissa breathlessly. 'Very impressive.'

'Good.' The older woman turned to wave an arm airily in the direction of the desk. 'This is Betty.'

Betty was a blonde in a low-cut blouse, with blood-red fingernails and lipstick to match. She was beautiful.

Melissa felt like Cinderella.

'Betty, this is my new assistant, Melissa Sutherland.'

Melissa saw the other girl's brows rise, and although Betty was too polite to show her real feelings, Melissa knew exactly what she was thinking.

Through a door was a long corridor with Vivienne's offices at the end. The woman sailed along like a queen, smiling graciously to any of the staff she happened to meet, with Melissa following behind trying not to appear too conspicuous, though painfully aware of the puzzled glances directed her way. Maybe it hadn't been such a good idea changing her image like this? She shrugged metaphorically. It was too late. There was not a thing she could do about it.

The outer office was Melissa's, Vivienne's leading from it. 'Beebee will be here shortly,' she said, disappearing through her door. 'Settle yourself in before the fun begins.'

Melissa had done no more than take the cover from her typewriter when the door opened and a whirlwind passed through. He was tall, black-haired, well dressed, and would have been good-looking if his lips weren't compressed, nor his brows knitted together in a frown.

She thought he had not seen her until, at the very last moment, he turned and directed an intensely piercing stare in her direction. It was designed to kill. The old Melissa would have challenged it but, already feeling less than confident, she lowered her eyes to her desk.

'Vivienne, who the hell is that?' He slammed the door so violently that it bounced open again, and no one bothered to close it.

And who the hell was he? wondered Melissa, her

hackles rising. How dared he speak about her in that
manner! And then she smiled. This was exactly the sort of
reaction she had been aiming for. It proved her disguise
had worked brilliantly.

'That's Melly, my new assistant. I did tell you about
her. Don't you approve?'

Melissa could picture the twinkle in Vivienne's eyes;
she could also imagine the condemnation in the man's.

'Approve? God, Vivienne, what is she? Another one of
your lame ducks?'

As she shamelessly listened to their conversation,
Melissa quivered with rage. Hearing herself described so
cruelly was making her blood boil.

'I had enough trying to get through to Pamela,' he said
harshly. 'Why do you always land them on me at times
like this? I need someone I can rely on. I can just imagine
what it will be like with that one out there.'

That one out there! Melissa did not know how she
stopped herself from rushing in.

'You seem to forget that she has to meet clients,
Vivienne,' he went on. 'You should let me interview
them. The company image demands a bright, attractive
girl with a sparkling personality, not a mouse-like
creature who looks as though she'd be frightened to say
boo to a goose.'

Melissa's fingers curled into fists and she sat down
heavily on her chair, breathing deeply. Who did he think
he was, telling Vivienne how to run her business? He
could only be one of her employees, perhaps a manager,
or a director even. But surely, surely to goodness, he had
no right speaking like that?

Suddenly the door was closed between them and their

voices fell to an inaudible level. Melissa's breathing gradually subsided and she busied herself looking through the files, trying to familiarise herself with the customer's names. She wished Beebee would arrive. Another woman would help soothe her rattled nerves.

It was a good half-hour before the door opened again. Melissa had sat twiddling her thumbs for most of that time, apart from taking a few phone calls, some of which Vivienne had accepted, while the rest were re-directed to the creative director.

Vivienne was all smiles, but the man's smile faded as he looked at Melissa. His eyes narrowed, and there was again that criticism he had directed at her when he first walked through the room.

'Melly, love, I'd like you to meet Benedict Burton. Beebee for short. And this, Beebee, is Melissa Sutherland, the daughter of a very dear friend of mine, and a very competent secretary.'

Melissa was horrified. This was Beebee? And she was expected to work with him for the next three days? It was not a woman, but a man. The despised sex. She couldn't. She wouldn't! But she was forgetting: he wasn't interested in her; he had made that very clear. All she had to do was be good at her job. There would be no unwelcome advances.

He nodded his head curtly in acknowledgement of Vivienne's introduction, but did not offer his hand. 'Have you experience in advertising, Miss Sutherland?'

Vivienne answered for her. 'No, she hasn't, but she's a quick learner, and I have no doubts that she'll fit in. And you can't call her Miss Sutherland. It's Melissa, or Melly if you prefer.'

Benedict Burton clearly had doubts about her

qualifications, many of them. His smoky grey eyes were taking in every inch of her, from the thick reddish-brown hair scraped back from her shining face, her eyes which looked smaller without mascara on her pale lashes, the shadows beneath them, her bloodless lips, the shift dress that hung shapelessly to her calves, right down to her feet in a pair of flat-heeled sandals.

Melissa caught Vivienne's eye and accepted the challenge. 'I'm sorry, Mr Burton—or may I call you Benedict?—if I don't exactly conform with the image you have in mind. I'll just have to make sure that my work more than compensates for my lack of—beauty.'

His lips thinned. 'It's nothing to do with me what you look like.'

'But I did hear you tell Aunt Viv that I looked like a mouse—or was it a lame duck? I'm not sure.' Melissa did not know what was driving her. She simply wanted to humiliate him as he had her.

Didn't you know that eavesdroppers never hear good of themselves?' His voice was ominously quiet, betraying his anger far more than if he had shouted.

'How could I help it, when the door was open, and your voice was loud enough to be heard in the street?'

'Children, children,' intervened Vivienne, 'I think that's enough.'

Melissa felt the blood rush to her cheeks. 'Oh, I'm sorry, Aunt Viv, I mean Viv. That was very rude. I don't know what came over me.'

The older woman smiled. 'I think I do. Beebee can be extremely overpowering. You'll soon get used to him.' And in a louder tone, 'Won't she, Beebee? Tell her your bark's worse than your bite.'

He merely grunted and turned back into Vivienne's office, this time closing the door firmly.

Vivienne shook her head, smiling broadly. 'I should have warned you about Beebee. He's a law unto himself. He's my godson; you must have heard me mention him?'

Melissa shook her head.

'He worked his way up in my business until eventually I made him my partner. I don't know what I'd do without him now. I love that boy.'

Boy? Melissa did not class him as a boy. He was a man, all man, as masculine as they come. Ruthless, arrogant, domineering. Nothing at all like Tim, who had always been gentle and considerate. And she did not see how she was going to work amicably with him for the next three days. Although, on the other hand, it might be fun proving that she was not the dimwit he had dubbed her.

'And now I must go.' Vivienne smiled fondly at the younger girl. 'You'll cope, I know you will. And the challenge will help you forget Tim.'

The challenge? The new job, or pitting herself against Benedict Burton? An involuntary smile curved Melissa's lips.

'That's better,' said Vivienne at once. 'Attagirl; he's really quite nice once you get to know him.'

After Vivienne had gone Melissa sat quietly waiting at her desk for the summons which she knew would come. She did not have to wait long.

Vivienne's office was in stark contrast to the luxurious trimmings of the reception area. The carpet was oatmeal, a black leather settee sat against one wall, the desk was black glass. There were one or two plants to bring the room to life, and several abstract paintings on the walls. But for all that it was a relaxing room. Except for the man sitting behind the desk!

He did not look entirely at ease there. It was not his type of room, Melissa could tell that, but he had his jacket off and his shirtsleeves rolled up and he handed a pile of letters to her for answering. 'I've scribbled notes on them. You can manage? You don't need me to dictate them?' His grey eyes met her green ones.

Melissa held his gaze. 'I'm sure I shall have no difficulty.' Her answer was quietly confident, although inside she was fuming. Vivienne had told him she was a competent secretary. Why did he talk down to her? Appearances should not make any difference.

Nor did she like the way he was looking at her. His gaze had left her face now and was skimming over her body, as if her shapeless dress did not exist and he was seeing her voluptuous curves beneath. A sudden warmth ran through her. She lifted her chin. 'Is that all?'

He inclined his head. 'For the moment.'

Briefly she noticed his black hair was turning grey at the temples. It looked at though it had been recently trimmed, quite short round his ears but shaped almost to his collar at the back. His jaw was clean-shaven but with a hint of blue still, and he wore a distinctive aftershave that she had not come across before. Woody, tangy, masculine. He was really quite attractive—and why was she thinking such a thing? She was not interested in him. She was interested in no man.

She turned and walked out of his office, conscious of his eyes still upon her. She wondered why he disapproved of her so strongly. Was it because he preferred girls who were pretty and vivacious—so that he could chat them up? Had he been looking forward to a brief affair with Vivienne's new secretary? Was that what was niggling him? She wondered whether he was married. She guessed so. He looked about thirty-five, and a man of his calibre, and with his physical attributes, would hardly remain single for long.

'One other thing, Miss Sutherland, don't put any calls through for the next hour.'

No 'please', just a bald statement. Melissa clamped her lips and got on with the letters. He had used a brown pen and his writing was bold and aggressive. She wondered what a graphologist would make of it. But she had no difficulty in deciphering his notes, and the pile of letters steadily rose.

The telephone rang frequently, but most callers, on learning that Vivienne Winters was out of the country, said they would ring back. One particularly irate man, though, insisted on speaking to Benedict Burton. She had no choice.

'A Mr Wellbeck, of Wellbeck Morton,' she said, putting him through.

A few minutes later the adjoining door crashed open and Benedict Burton glared so fiercely that Melissa's heart stopped altogether for a few seconds. 'Weren't my instructions clear?' His tone was clipped and very angry.

'Perfectly,' she said, determined to remain cool and polite.

'Then why did you put that damned man through?'

'He was most insistent. I had no choice,' she said reasonably.

'And I gave you a simple order. What's the matter with you, girl? Are you incapable of following basic instructions?'

Melissa clenched her teeth. There was plenty she would

like to say to this hateful man but this was not the time nor the place.

'Cat got your tongue, eh? I suggest in future you listen a little more intently to what I have to say.'

He went back into the office before Melissa's blood quite boiled. She wondered whether he would have spoken to her so rudely had she been herself, instead of disguised like a frump. Somehow she doubted it. Men like him always made excuses for pretty girls. Beautiful girls didn't need brains. God, they made her sick.

She had scarcely begun typing when her intercom went yet again. 'I'd like a coffee,' he barked. 'Black, no sugar.'

Melissa pulled a rude face at the instrument and stood up. She had already spotted a kettle and cups in a little restroom adjoining the offices and it took her no more than a few minutes to fix his drink.

When she entered his office he did not even acknowledge her presence. She set the cup down on his desk, feeling a childish desire to throw it over him. What a disagreeable, mannerless person he was.

She had reached the door when a curt, 'Thank you,' sounded after her. An afterthought, no doubt. She glanced back but his attention was on the computer screen in front of him.

She settled down to her letters, but a few short minutes later he sent for her again. 'Do you know how to work one of these things?' he growled.

Melissa held back her smile with difficulty, glad she had familiarised herself with the terminal in her office. 'Yes, Mr Burton.'

Her polite response seemed to annoy him even more. He stood over her as she punched the appropriate keys and Melissa could not ignore his total masculinity. It sailed over and through her in little shockwaves, and it worried her that she found him attractive. He really was a most disturbing man.

When she had retrieved the information he desired she stood up.

'Thank you, Melissa.'

She eyed him guardedly, her green eyes wide, completely unaware that there was no disguising their beauty, even without the artifice of mascara and eyeshadow. Had she gone up a peg in his estimation? His grey eyes were narrowed as they looked at her, but there was still no sign of friendliness, and she mentally shrugged.

She was thankful that he then left her severely alone until lunchtime, and she looked forward to getting out for a much-needed breath of fresh air. Benedict Burton was claustrophobic.

But her plans were doomed when he called her into his office. 'We'll have a sandwich lunch here so that I can go through the various projects with you. As Viv's assistant you'll need to know almost as much as she does. Think you're up to it?

Melissa chin rose characteristically. 'Of course. But I had made other plans. I need some fresh air. I intended going for a walk along the riverbank.'

'Then you'll have to change your plans, young lady,' he snapped brutally. 'If you're going to learn the business then you haven't time to go wandering about outside.'

'But it is my lunch hour.'

'Are you meeting someone?'

She shook her head.

'Then your argument is not valid. Believe me, you'll need to learn as quickly as possible if you value your job.'

Her brows rose. 'Vivienne's my boss, not you.'

'Vivienne's a soft touch,' he scorned.

'Meaning?' she questioned coldly.

His eyes met hers. 'You wanted to move away from home—you needed a job—you're as close to her as family. So she gave you one, regardless of whether you were suitable.'

Melissa tensed inside, unable to credit that he knew so much about her. 'She's told you—about me?'

'No more than I've just revealed,' he admitted tersely.

Relief! 'And you think I can't do the job?'

'That remains to be seen.'

Melissa's back stiffened. 'I'll fetch the sandwiches.' She would soon show him that she was not the idiot he thought her. God, what an insufferable man he was.

Betty in reception told her about the little shop around the corner. 'How are you getting on with Mr Burton?'

It was a perfectly innocent queston, but Melissa knew what the girl was thinking. 'As well as can be expected.'

'You'll have to watch him. He has quite a reputation.'

Something told Melissa that he had already propositioned Betty, and probably he had got much further than he ever would with her. Betty looked like the proverbial dumb blonde. The type men understood!

Melissa fetched the sandwiches, hoping he liked turkey or ham, which was all they had left, and returned to her office. She boiled water and made tea, loaded it all on to a tray and went in to him.

He glanced up absently. He looked tired, she thought. For an instant he seemed surprised to see her, then he smiled.

It was the first time she had seen him smile and it was amazing the difference it made to his face, warming his eyes, dispelling the harshness, making him almost human.

The next hour went so quickly that Melissa was truly astonished. They munched their way through the sandwiches, drank a potful of tea, and she listened while he explained each and every one of the campaigns Vivienne was currently working on.

He made it sound so interesting that Melissa forgot her antipathy, relaxing for the first time in his company, listening avidly, throwing in the odd question, seeing the occasional surprise in his eyes.

When the pot was empty and the plates were clean and he had finished talking, she stood up. He rose, too, and rested his hand on her shoulder. 'An hour well spent, don't you agree?'

Melissa backed hastily. Had he seen through her disguise already? Was Vivienne right when she said her beauty still shone through? One touch, one softly spoken word, one kiss, that was all it took. And she was not ready. She was ready for no man, not yet. Not for a long time.

And yet he really was attractive, she was forced to admit. Not handsome in the true sense of the word. His face was rugged and hard-boned, he was tall and physically fit, virile, very masculine, the sort most women turned their heads to look at twice. Nothing at all like Tim who, though tall, did not have Benedict's build, and whose face was boyish. He could never dominate like this man.

Benedict frowned fiercely. 'What the hell's wrong? I'm not about to force myself on you.'

Melissa swallowed hard. 'I know, but I don't want you to touch me.'

His eyes narrowed. 'Why? Is it a man you're running away from? Is that the reason for this——' he drew the shape of her in the air '—this ridiculous garb? Are you trying to make yourself as unattractive as possible?'

Melissa lifted her chin. 'I don't know what you're talking about, Mr Burton.'

'Oh, come, Melissa, I wasn't born yesterday. Admittedly at first sight I was—put off, to say the least, but now I've had time to study you I can see that you're nothing like the image you're trying to portray.'

'How do you know it's an image?' demanded Melissa crossly. 'How do you know I don't look like this all the time?'

His thick brows rose. 'If you do, then it's a waste of a beautiful woman.'

'Maybe it's the way I want to be,' she snapped.

'But it's not how I want you to be.'

Melissa nodded. 'The image is bad for the company, is that what you're saying? Vivienne didn't raise any objections.'

'Vivienne's a woman,' he snarled. 'I like beautiful girls around me, Melissa, girls who know how to dress, how to make the most of themselves, and that's what our clients like, too. I don't want to see you like this in the office tomorrow.'

She eyed him haughtily, seeing the truth in what he said, but resenting the way he spoke to her. 'And if I'm no different?'

He smiled grimly. 'Then I shall take you home and dress you myself.'

Melissa went warm at the thought, every nerve-end tingling. He would, too. But still she stood her ground. 'I am what I am, Mr Burton. I'm sorry if you disapprove.'

Soon afterwards Benedict Burton returned to his own office somewhere else in the building and Melissa was left to herself. How peaceful it suddenly was. She half expected him to come and see how she was coping, but at five he had still made no appearance and, as one of the juniors had collected her post, she slipped away.

When she got home she took a good look at the house and spotted an entrance door at the side that had not been there the last time she visited Vivienne. Obviously this was Benedict Burton's private entrance. She let her gaze go up to the top-floor windows. They looked blankly back down at her. Was he home yet? she wondered.

Shaking her head, she let herself into the house, going straight up to her room and stripping off ready for a shower. When Vivienne had first told her she would be away for a few days it had not unduly disturbed her, but now she knew Benedict Burton was living upstairs, might even at this moment be in the room directly above her, Melissa felt nervous and a shiver ran through her.

She was cross with herself for thinking about him, yet she could not get him out of her mind. Had she known about him she would certainly never have taken the job. It was the fact that she had thought she would be working solely for a woman that had appealed to her.

The doorbell rang as she stepped out of the shower. At first Melissa was tempted to ignore it, but when it rang again more persistently she pulled on her short towelling robe and ran down the stairs.

She opened the door a mere two inches and nearly died when she saw Benedict Burton standing there. 'What the hell do you want?' On her home ground she felt she could speak to him however she liked.

'To take you to dinner,' he answered pleasantly. A smile even accompanied his words.

Melissa felt suspicious. 'Why?'

'Because you're alone, and in a strange place, and I thought you might like some company.'

'Not yours,' she said positively. He had changed out of the dark suit he had worn all day into a very pale blue one, with a white silk shirt and a spotted tie. The light material enhanced his tan and made him look taller and broader and infinitely more dangerous. She had never met a man quite like him.

'I don't issue invitations to all and sundry,' he clipped, his smile abruptly disappearing.

'Just to gauche girls with no dress sense?' she thrust, and began to shut the door.

His lips thinned and he moved quickly. Melissa's strength was pitifully weak compared to his. The door was open and he was inside before she could do a thing about it.

'How dare you?' she cried, pulling her robe more tightly about her, acutely conscious of her nakedness beneath. 'How dare you? Just because you're my aunt's partner and godson, and just because you live in her flat, it doesn't give you the right to march in here whenever you feel like it!'

CHAPTER TWO

BENEDICT BURTON smiled insolently. 'Don't look so affronted. I'm sure it's not the first time you've been caught dressed in so little.'

That was true. Tim had been in and out of their house so often, she had never worried about trying to impress him. He was almost like one of the family. But this man was different. He was a stranger for one thing, and a very disturbing one at that. And she was trying to run away from men, not right into the hands of the first one she met.

'You have a nerve,' she spat. 'I didn't invite you in here and I don't want you. Please go.'

'You've already eaten? If that's so then we can——'

'We can do nothing,' she cut in sharply. 'I intend spending my evening alone, completely alone.'

'That's a pity.' His gaze probed the V of her robe, then wandered shamelessly down the length of her legs. An impossible heat pervaded Melissa's skin. Lord, what a nerve this man had! Was Vivienne aware what he was like? Had she known he would come chasing her at the first opportunity? How was she going to get rid of him?

She held the door wide. 'Get out!'

His eyes met and held hers. 'The lady sounds as though she means it.'

'I do,' she snapped.

He lifted his shoulders. 'And I was looking forward to an—entertaining evening. You're different, Melissa. You intrigue me. Oh, well, you can't win them all.' And to her surprise he turned and left.

The moment she had closed the door Melissa let out a ragged breath. She felt weak at the knees and totally confused. What sort of game was he playing? It had to be a game; he couldn't really be interested in her. Or could he? Was she a challenge? Had she, by trying to make herself unattractive, drawn even more attention to herself?

She returned slowly to her bedroom and studied her face critically in the mirror. She saw what he had seen: a girl in her early twenties, tall, a clear skin, flushed at this moment, wide-spaced eyes—ignore the shadows—a nose that erred on the large side.

She let the robe fall. A tiny waist, slender hips, long legs. These were her good points. On the minus side were her ample breasts, her too wide mouth, her much too high forehead. She hated her hair off her face.

With a savage gesture she pulled out the pins and it tumbled in thick luxurious waves about her face and shoulders. What a difference it made.

She swung her head, loving the silky feel of it against her naked shoulders and breasts. She wondered what it would feel like if Benedict touched her in these self-same places, then cried out aloud in disgust. What was happening to her?'

She had only just finished with Tim, for heaven's sake! She had been cruelly jilted on her wedding eve, her heart broken, and she had sworn never to look at another man. And yet here she was thinking about Benedict Burton, all thoughts of Tim gone. She was out of her mind.

Unable to face the thought of food, Melissa attempted to watch television, but it was impossible. She could not get Benedict out of her mind. It would have been different were he not in the same building, but she kept thinking about him up there, wondering what he was doing, what sort of thoughts were going through his mind. In the end she went early to bed.

But she could not sleep. She lay awake listening for sounds above her, still unable to rid her mind of him. Eventually she did drop off, but her sleep was disturbed by a nightmare that had grown all too familiar in recent weeks. She woke sweating and screaming and hoping that he had not heard.

This same nightmare had dogged her nearly every single night since Tim had called the wedding off. It seemed to have nothing to do with Tim, and yet it was only then that it had started.

She dreamt that she was flying, her arms spread like a soaring bird, trying to escape from someone, some faceless, nameless being, who all the time was getting closer and closer. Then suddenly she fell like a stone, down and down, the ground rushing up to meet her with terrifying speed. Always she woke up before actually hitting the ground, but every time she had the dream she was a yard or two nearer. One day she might not make it!

She scolded herself for letting her imagination run away with her and took a cooling shower. Then she went downstairs into the kitchen and made a pot of tea.

After drinking several cups she returned to her room and got ready for work. Back went her hair, on went the same straight shift, her face scrubbed shining clean. Her mouth lifted impishly at the corners. Intrigued, are you,

Mr Burton? Well, here I come again, plain and sexless and ready for battle.

He was in before her. The black car growled ferociously in the car park. She knew instinctively that it was his, and she felt like giving its gleaming black paintwork a kick. It was like its owner, all smooth and polished—inviting a second glance.

The lift took her swiftly upwards. She smiled a good morning to Betty, nodded to all the other nameless faces, and strode into her office.

She had done no more than take the cover from her typewriter when the internal telephone buzzed. Melissa had not even realised he was in there, presuming he would be in his own office. She would have liked a few minutes to pat her hair into place and sort herself out. It was not even nine o'clock.

'Miss Sutherland, bring your notebook in please.'

The tone of his voice was deeper over the intercom. It sent a shiver down her spine. She picked up her pad and pencil and walked in.

His eyes were on the door waiting for her, and they narrowed dangerously when he saw that she had made no attempt to alter her appearance. But to her surprise he said nothing, merely indicated a chair at the side of his desk—where he could see every inch of her.

Melissa sat down and demurely tugged her dress over her knees, an action which did not go unnoticed by him. 'This is to be drafted out on the word processor,' he said. 'You can use it?'

She nodded.

But whether he was impressed she had no idea. Once he began dictating, though, she had no time to think about Benedict the man. She had a feeling he was testing her. He went on and on, page after page of a long, complicated schedule, but she got down every word and was with him to the end.

'I'd like that finished before lunch,' he said, dismissing her.

'Yes, sir.'

He frowned. 'Don't get smart with me, Miss Sutherland.'

What a changed man from last night. Had he accepted that she wanted nothing to do with him? She shrugged mentally. 'I was merely being polite.'

There was no answer as she left his room but she could feel his eyes boring into her back.

Had she been left alone Melissa would have completed the work. But the phone rang incessantly, people came in and out asking her questions she could not answer, she was constantly having to search through the files, and it was such a hectic morning that she was only half-way through the schedule at a quarter past twelve when he emerged from Vivienne's office.

He looked at her expectantly, studied the screen and then frowned. 'I'm sorry,' she said, 'I've had so many interruptions that ——'

'It was too much for you?'

'Certainly not,' she defended, the derogatory tone of his voice needing her. 'And if it's all that important I'll work through my lunch hour to finish it.'

'You'd better,' he said. 'The client is coming at two to go through it.'

Which he could have told her in the beginning, she fumed. She was hungry. Having had no dinner last night and no breakfast this morning, she had been looking foward to one of those delicious brown bread sandwiches they had enjoyed yesterday. There would be no time to fetch one now.

However, at least with everyone out at lunch there were no interruptions, and the schedule was completed and printed out by one-thirty. She placed it on his desk, and decided she might still have time to run out for a sandwich after all.

At the door, though, she met Benedict returning. 'Ah, Miss Sutherland—you've finished?'

She nodded.

'Good. I'd like to dictate some letters before Mr Hennessy arrives. Bring in your notebook.'

'But——'

Her interruption went unheeded. He marched into Vivienne's office and she was given no choice but to follow.

He did not stop until Betty rang through to say that his client had arrived. 'I'd like those to catch tonight's post,' he said.

Which meant there would be no lunch for her today, fumed Melissa. Hadn't he realised that? Didn't he care? Damn the man!

Their creative director, Bill Warner, and Mr Hennessy, one of the directors from Drew and Co, a leading firm of jewellers, arrived at her office and she showed them through.

She finished the letters and did some filing from yesterday, made coffee for the visitors, and took numerous telephone calls. At five they still hadn't emerged. Benedict had said he wanted his letters to go today. Dared she interrupt?

Mentally squaring her shoulders, she tapped on his door

and popped her head round. 'Mr Burton, can you sign your letters please?'

To her surprise he smiled and beckoned her in and he looked in a good humour. Obviously all was going well. She stood patiently while he scrawled his signature on each of the pages, conscious of the scrutiny of the other two men.

When he had finished she picked them up and walked towards the door.

'Miss Sutherland.' Benedict's voice called her back. 'See if you can find Drew's last schedule. It was two or three years back. It should be with the old files in that cupboard in your office.'

She folded the letters and put them in their envelopes, rang for the junior to collect them, and then opened the door to the cupboard. It was jam-packed full of files and they did not seem to be in any sort of order, as though each time someone had taken one out they had pushed it back in again anywhere. There seemed nothing for it but to go through them systematically.

When Benedict's door opened and his visitors filed out she had still not found it. 'Never mind,' said Mr Hennessy kindly. 'Tomorrow will do. I'm sure it's long past your going home time.'

But Benedict thought differently. 'No, I'd like that file tonight, Miss Sutherland.'

He face was flushed and a couple of pins had come out of her hair, and she could cheerfully have flung each of the files at him, one by one. But somehow she managed to smile. 'Of course, Mr Burton.'

Bill Warner's lips lifted at the corners. He had not missed the undercurrents. She liked Bill. He had been in and out of her office several times these last two days and always had a cheerful word.

Once he was rid of his visitors Benedict returned to her office. She was reaching a file from the topmost shelf and did not hear him enter. His voice startled her and she dropped the file, a flood of others following. Soon she was surrounded by an avalanche of papers.

She swung round angrily and the last pins came out of her hair so that it tumbled in heavy chestnut waves about her shoulders. She heard Benedict's indrawn breath and looking at him through the curtain of her hair she saw him step towards her.

In that moment Melissa felt hypnotised.

'It's beautiful,' he said, 'quite beautiful.' And he reached out a hand, threading her hair through his fingers, feeling it, treating it as reverently as if it were home-spun silk. 'I want you to wear it like this, always.'

Melissa suffered his touch for a few seconds, no more. 'I'll wear my hair how I want to,' she snapped and, jerking away, she bent down on the pretext of gathering up some of the papers. In those few moments she had felt so aware of him it was unbelievable.

'Melissa, stand up.'

She pretended she had not heard. Surely he had seen a girl with long hair before?

'Melissa.' There was a warning note in his tone now.

Taking a deep breath Melissa stood up, but too quickly. The room spun around and Benedict's steadying hands saved her from falling.

For a few seconds she felt the hardness of his chest, the strength of his arms, and could smell the male scent of him. And for a crazy moment she wanted to stop there.

The next second she was struggling to escape. What insanity! 'I'm all right,' she protested loudly, too loudly perhaps.

'What brought that about?' A frown creased his brow.

Melissa glared belligerantly. 'You should know. It's your fault I worked through my lunch hour.'

He looked at her thoughtfully. 'When was the last time you ate?'

She shrugged. 'Yesterday lunchtime.'

He cursed loudly. 'How stupid can you get? What happened to dinner last night?'

'I wasn't hungry.'

'And breakfast?'

'I never eat breakfast. But I was going to have some lunch,' she claimed accusingly.

He let out a deep sigh. 'Come on, I'll take you home. You're in no fit state to drive yourself.'

'No, thank you.' Melissa shook her head wildly, then wished she hadn't as another spell of dizziness overtook her.

Benedict muttered an oath beneath his breath and, gripping her arm, led her protestingly from the room, giving her time only to pick up her bag.

The black monster awaited. But when she sank down into the deep leather seat it wasn't a monster after all. She leaned back and closed her eyes, then jerked upright when his arm brushed her breast. But all he was doing was reaching for her seatbelt.

'I can manage,' she said sharply. His touch, though light, felt as though it had seared her skin.

Her unwitting response puzzled her. Why, when she had been so badly hurt, and not all that long ago either, when she had decided that no man was to be trusted, was she feeling like this?

She closed her eyes again and tried to ignore him, though it was difficult when his whole presence filled the car. Each time he changed gear she was aware of his hand coming that little bit closer, and her leg muscles tensed; and there was a faint spicy scent of aftershave filling her nostrils.

'Are you all right?' His voice penetrated her thoughts.

She nodded without opening her eyes.

The journey to Vivienne's house took no more than a few minutes, yet it felt like an hour. Melissa was greatly relieved when at last the car stopped.

She was quite capable of getting out and walking into the house, but Benedict insisted on taking her arm. She wondered whether he was aware of what his touch did to her.

'For an intelligent girl,' he rasped, 'you're not very clever when it comes to looking after yourself. You look as though you haven't eaten properly for weeks.'

Which was true. Ever since Tim had jilted her she had only pecked at her food. Her mother had tried to make her eat but it stuck in her throat and tasted like sawdust.

'I suggest you go and change out of that awful dress, and if I were you I'd dispose of it, unless you want me to do it for you. Where the hell did you find it?'

'It's my defence—against men like you,' she shot angrily, unwisely.

His brows arched. 'Oh, no, Melissa; whatever I am, I don't go around frightening little girls. That sure is a mountain-sized chip you have on your shoulder. One day I'm going to find out what it's all about. Meantime, while you're changing, I'll cook us a meal.'

Melissa looked at him, horrified. 'There's no need.' She did not want him staying here. Eight hours a day in the office was more than enough.

'I think there is,' he said grimly. 'I want to make sure that you eat.'

He was treating her like a child! It made her angry. 'I don't need you to look after me, Mr Burton.'

'Benedict,' he said mildly, 'if you don't mind, and I intend cooking a meal no matter what you say—so you're only wasting your breath.'

Melissa glared then bounced upstairs, stripped off, and stood for several angry minutes beneath the shower. Who the hell did he think he was? What right had he intruding where he was not wanted?

She rubbed herself dry furiously and deliberated what to wear. In the end she chose a straight white skirt and a yellow chiffon blouse, that was loose-fitting enough to hide her curves, yet which had an attractive scoop neckline. Determinedly though she scraped her hair back and tied it with a yellow ribbon into a ponytail.

She looked a bit better than her image she had presented at the office, but still not as attractive as she knew she could look.

When she went back downstairs Benedict was in the kitchen. Steaks were sizzling, as was a pan of chipped potatoes, and a bowl of salad stood to one side.

He eyed her up and down, calmly taking in every inch of her from her high-heeled sandal-clad feet, up the length of her bare lightly tanned legs, over her hips skimmed by the white linen, lingering fractionally on the faint thrust of her breasts through the delicate material of her blouse, finally coming to rest on her simmering green eyes.

His scrutiny set her nerve-ends tingling, but it also made her angry, and she tossed her head. 'If you've quite finished.'

His lips twisted in a secret smile. 'Not quite.' He moved towards her, and before she could guess at his intentions reached out and released her hair from its ribbon.

Too late Melissa tried to stop him.

'I thought I asked you to wear it loose.' There was a low throbbing tone to his voice and a look in his eyes which disturbed her.

'I don't have to do what you say.' She nervously ran the tip of her tongue over her lips.

His eyes narrowed and his hands reached out to her, his fingers feeling the thickness of her hair. He seemed to find it irresistible. Then he cupped her face between his hands looking deep into the green of her eyes. Melissa held herself tense. This was too impossible for words. She shouldn't be feeling like this.

'I don't know what sort of a man it was who made you like this,' he rasped harshly, 'but it's about time you snapped out of it.'

His fingers traced the contours of her face, her eyebrows, her eyelids, the shadows beneath them, the straight line of her nose, her cheekbones, her mouth.

Her lips trembled. Crazily she wanted to ensnare his hands in her own, to press kisses into his palms, and on his fingertips. To have him kiss her! And she was angry with herself for even entertaining such a thought.

'You're really quite beautiful, Melissa. It's criminal to hide behind a facade of ugliness.'

She eyed him aggressively, deliberately stemming the

tremors that raced through her. 'Don't try to flatter me, Mr Burton.' She had to say 'mister'. It put that barrier between them, the barrier she so desperately needed.

'I'm speaking the truth, as you well know.'

She clapped her hands to her ears, swinging away from him, unaware that his fingers had returned to her hair and that she was ensnared in her own silken trap.

'Are you afraid of me, Melissa?' His voice rumbled from deep in his throat as inch by inch he pulled her back round and towards him, winding her hair slowly round his hands, his eyes never leaving hers.

'Why should I be?' Her voice rose in a tiny squeak. Not afraid! Aware. Too much so. And too soon. She didn't want to get involved, not with anyone, not yet—perhaps not ever.

'There's no reason,' he said softly, 'no reason at all, unless it's of your own making.' Only centimetres now separated them.

Somehow Melissa managed to drag her eyes away from his. He saw too much, far too much. He must never guess what he did to her. This was not in her plan of things at all. Oh, Vivienne, she cried silently, why did you have to go away right now?

'I think the steak's burning,' he said, letting go of her abruptly, but not before she had seen the ghost of a smile tugging at his lips. He knew, damn him. He knew!

It was an excellent meal, but although Melissa had felt desperately hungry she ate no more than half of what he put in front of her. Having eaten so little these last weeks, she found a few mouthfuls filled her up.

While they were eating Benedict discussed with her the Drew campaign he had been working on all day.

'Hennessy wasn't too keen on some of my suggestions,' he admitted surprisingly. 'He kept harping back to something Viv did several years ago. But I don't see why we should do a carbon copy. People have long memories when it comes to commercials. They don't want to see the same ones screened year after year.'

'Is that the reason you wanted the file?'

He nodded.

'Can I make a suggestion?' she asked hesitantly.

His brows rose and he waited.

She hoped he wouldn't consider her impertinent. 'I realise I don't know anything about this sort of thing, not yet, but from a woman's point of view I think jewellery should be filmed in a more—romantic situation. Just showing it off on a woman isn't enough.'

'Really, Miss Sutherland? Do go on. I'm sure my fifteen years' experience hardly counts for anything against your far superior wisdom.'

'That's not fair,' protested Melissa. 'It was just a thought. I'm probably completely wrong, but, well——'

'Perhaps you'd like to think some more about it? Perhaps you'd like to go through all the other campaigns we're working on and see what you think about them?'

His tone was bitter and she could not blame him. 'I'm sorry,' she whispered, 'I should never have said anything.'

There was silence then until the end of the meal. They took their coffee into the lounge. 'A liqueur?' he asked gruffly. 'A brandy perhaps?'

Melissa shook her head. They'd had wine with their meal and it had done nothing to get rid of her light-headedness.

'You still look pale. How are you feeling?'

'Much better,' she said with determined brightness, convinced he did not really care. 'You can go now. There's no need for you to stay any longer.'

His brows shot up in that manner she was beginning to know so well. 'I'm not sure you're in any fit state to be left alone.'

Melissa felt faint alarm.

'Viv would expect me to look after you.'

Viv would expect it of him! And she had thought he was interested in her. How wrong could one be? 'Viv's not here,' she cried.

'Exactly. If you're ill in the night, who's to see to your needs?'

'I don't need you as nursemaid,' she protested angrily. 'I'm not ill. I was faint with hunger, that's all.'

'And you've eaten about enough to fill a sparrow. Don't be foolish, Melissa. I'm staying.'

'You're not!'

He drew in a harsh breath. 'What the hell's wrong with you?' he demanded. 'Are you still afraid of me?'

'I never was,' she claimed. Of herself, maybe, not him.

He shook his head, as though never in a month of Sundays would he be able to understand her. 'Very well, I'll go up to my flat.'

She heaved a sigh of relief.

'But to be on the safe side I intend unlocking the communicating door at the end of your landing.'

Melissa's eyes shot wide open.

'Normally it is never opened,' he continued. 'Vivienne and I lead our own lives. She had a separate entrance and staircase installed for that very reason. But I think tonight it would be advisable.'

'In case I call out for you?' she asked drily. 'You haven't a cat in hell's chance of that.'

'Nevertheless, the door will be open,' he said firmly. 'I'm going out into the garden for some air. Do you want to come?'

Melissa shook her head and the moment he disappeared went up to her room. She looked out and saw him in the fast fading light. On the horizon the sky was blood-red, silhouetting his shape so that he was no more than a shadow. She had no idea whether he was looking her way or not, until she saw him raise his hand in a mock salute.

Damn! She hoped he didn't think she was looking at him. It was Vivienne's garden she was admiring, inhaling the heady perfume of the honeysuckle beneath her window.

She undressed, pulled on a nightshirt and hurriedly climbed into bed. It was too early for sleep but at least she was rid of Benedict. And although she did not like the idea of the door between the main part of the house and his flat being unlocked, there was nothing she could do about it. She believed him when he said he would not harm her. But he was a man! That was enough. Thank goodness there was only one more day before Vivienne returned. Surely she could cope until then?

It was a long time before sleep claimed her. She lay listening for Benedict but heard nothing, and had no idea whether he was in bed, too, or still wandering around outside.

In the night her nightmare returned, and she woke to the sound of her own screams. The ground! She had hit the ground, the breath knocked out of her body, every bone crushed. She could not move. She could not see. She was dead.

'Melissa! Melissa, wake up.'

A man's urgent voice penetrated her unconsciousness. *'Melissa!'*

She was being shaken gently but firmly. She wasn't dead! She wasn't dead after all. She struggled to open her eyes, dazzled by an overhead light. Benedict Burton's blurred and anxious face was only inches from hers.

'Get away! Get away! What are you doing here?' He had his arms around her and they were on the floor. What the hell was he playing at?

'Shh, Melissa, you were dreaming. You had a nightmare. You fell out of bed.'

'You had no right coming down here. How dare you! What were you after?'

His lips tightened impatiently. 'Your screams were enough to raise the dead. I should think the whole street heard you. What was I supposed to do, ignore them?'

She frowned, memory returning. This was the night it had finally happened. But she wasn't dead after all. She was alive, and this man was holding her. She was soaked with perspiration and she was shivering, but she was alive. It was Tim who had been chasing her! She knew that now. But he hadn't wanted to catch her. He hadn't wanted her. He had let her go. He had let her fall down into space. And this man had taken her into his arms and saved her!

She crumpled suddenly, trying to fight back sudden tears. She had not cried when Tim jilted her. She had been too angry. But now they spilled, pouring down her cheeks, mingling with the sweat, running down Benedict's bare chest, making the dark hairs glisten like diamonds.

Diamonds? On a man's chest? Ludicrous! But in a commercial? Waiting for a woman to claim them? She could just see a woman's hand sliding sexily over the hard, muscular wall of his chest, inch by inch, until she found her prize. Would it work? Dare she suggest it? She laughed out loud, loudly and hysterically. And Benedict slapped her face.

It was like a douche of cold water. Her eyes snapped wide and she fought to free herself. He lifted her to her fèet. 'I'm sorry I had to to that.'

Was he? *Was he?* She cowered back like a hunted animal. 'Please go.' She had begun to shiver violently.

He swore loudly and fetched a huge bathsheet from the adjoining shower-room. 'Here, dry yourself on that. Where are your clean nighties?'

For pity's sake, he wasn't going to help her?

'In that drawer.'

He picked out the first one he came to. Flimsy and sheer. He held it up, looking from it to her, and back again. 'Something tells me, Melissa, that this is the real you. A very feminine and very sexy young woman. I'm looking forward to meeting her.'

With that he tossed the nightie on the bed and walked out of the room.

CHAPTER THREE

MELISSA stripped off her damp nightshirt and cocooned herself in the towel, her arms folded about her trembling body. The room felt empty now he had gone, and lonely, and she wished she hadn't been so eager to get rid of him.

She sat on the edge of the bed, rocking backwards and forwards, rocking, rocking, and gradually she felt calmer. The nightmare faded and all that was left were thoughts of Benedict.

It had felt good in his arms; there was no denying that. Although she had instinctively struggled to escape, she now regretted that she had fought him so fiercely. There was comfort to be gained from him.

Eventually she pulled the nightie over her head and crawled back into bed. She soon grew warm and her eyes closed and she knew no more until her musical alarm gently woke her the next morning.

In the light of day she decided that she had done the right thing in sending Benedict away. Moods were different in the middle of the night; she might well have got carried away. Benedict, too. It did not bear thinking about.

She jumped out of bed and yawned and stretched, and in the wardrobe mirror caught her reflection in the ridiculous wisp of sheer nylon. He thought this was the real Melissa Sutherland, did he? She smiled to herself.

It looked sexy, certainly. She had originally bought if for her wedding night!

At this point in her thoughts her smile faded and she tore at the nightdress with angry fingers. After showering she dressed in a plain grey skirt and a white blouse—short-sleeved, with a conventional collar, the floppy black bow at the neck its only concession to femininity. She hesitated over her hair then determinedly fixed it in a loose knot in her nape.

To her annoyance she found Benedict in the kitchen, and her eyes flashed hostilely. 'What are you doing here?'

'What does it look like?' he countered easily. 'I'm cooking breakfast.'

'You think I'm incapable?'

'No, but you're stupid enough to go without any.'

'And is this how it's to be, you coming in here whenever you feel like it?' she demanded. 'I insist that you go back up to your flat and lock the communicating door. Now!'

He sighed heavily. 'You know as well as I do that Viv will be back this afternoon. Besides what would I do with all this scrambled egg and toast? Take it up with me? Stop being unreasonable, Melissa. This is by far the best arrangement. Sit down. It's almost ready.'

She did as she was asked and in a few seconds he joined her. 'How are you feeling,' he asked, 'apart from being bad-tempered?'

Melissa shrugged. 'All right.' And grudgingly added, 'I'm sorry if I disturbed you last night.'

'Think nothing of it,' he said lightly. 'I half expected you might need me. That's why I unlocked the door.'

'Are you sure it wasn't because Vivienne would expect

you to look after me?' she asked sharply, more sharply than she had intended.

His brows rose. 'What reason would you have liked for me to leave the door open?'

He looked amused and Melissa snapped, 'I didn't want you to unlock it at all.'

'But you're glad I did?'

She lifted her shoulders. She would be lying if she said no. He had offered her comfort when she'd needed it, and he had gone when she asked him to. He had behaved like a perfect gentleman. 'I suppose so.'

'Such grudging gratitude. Would you like to pour the tea?'

Melissa was glad to have something to do, though she could not ignore the warmth that was seeping under her skin. There was something about sitting this close to Benedict that set her nerve ends tingling. He smelled fresh, his hair was still damp from the shower, and as yet he had not put on his tie.

She could see the dark hairs on the hard wall of his chest and recalled that last night she had been held firmly against it. Her hand trembled slightly as she filled his cup and she knew he lifted his eyes to her face. Did he know how much he was beginning to affect her?

'Sugar? Milk? she enquired huskily.

'As it comes,' he said.

She poured milk into her own and a half-spoonful of sugar and stirred and stirred until his hand stopped her.

'Penny for them, Melissa?'

She had been lost in thought, wondering why it was that she was beginning to think less and less about Tim and more and more about this man. She meant nothing to him, she knew that. She was a source of amusement, of irritation perhaps, she had aroused his curiosity, but that was about all. He was keeping his eye on her for Vivienne's sake. Once Vivienne returned, that door would be locked and she would have nothing more to do with him.

'They're worth far more than that,' she joked, 'but they're not for sale.'

'Pity.' And he looked as though he meant it.

She heaped scrambled egg on to a slice of toast and under Benedict's watchful eye managed to eat every bit. But she was glad when they had finished and she could leave the table.

Benedict pushed back his chair at the same time. 'If you're ready, we'll leave.'

Melissa had forgotten her car was still at the office and she would be travelling with him. Her dismay showed on her face.

He frowned. 'You don't like me, do you, Melissa? You don't like men at all.'

With a tiny smile and a shrug Melissa said, 'Not very much.'

'What happened, to make you like this?'

She eyed him coolly. 'Nothing I'd care to discuss.' Nothing at all really, just her whole life in ruins, wasted. Every year she had spent with Tim, loving him, wanting him, had been for nothing. There had never been any other man. She had wanted no one else. And that was the one thing that had not changed. She wanted no other man. She was not interested in Benedict Burton. Was she?

She swung away. 'I'll get my bag.' And ran up to her

room.

There were two spots of high colour in her cheeks and she made herself take several deep steadying breaths before she slowly made her way back down.

He was waiting in the hall, fully dressed now with tie and jacket. It was as if he, too, had shrugged off his other image, and she was glad because she wasn't ready for anything else yet. This was Benedict the businessman, and with him she could cope.

The journey was short and silent, and once back in the office his tenderness of the night before might never have existed. He barked orders at her, was furious when she accidentally cut off an important call, and he kept her going at full speed all morning.

But today she was determined to have her lunch hour and she slipped quietly out at one o'clock precisely. She bought a packet of sandwiches, and sat on the grass by the river. She threw crumbs to the ducks and almost forgot the time. When she returned, Benedict was in her office.

'Where the hell have you been?' His face was taut with anger, his grey eyes cold.

Melissa firmed her chin and looked him straight in the eye. 'Eating my lunch.'

'You should have told me you were going out.'

Was that a slight softening of his expression? She doubted it. A trick of the light perhaps. 'Why, so that you could have detained me?'

'Actually, I would have joined you.' His answer surprised her.

'Then it's a good job I didn't tell you, because I wanted to be alone.'

He looked at her long and hard, then lifted his

shoulders and walked away.

Later that afternoon Vivienne returned and Melissa was more than pleased to see her.

'How are you managing?' Vivienne's smile was warm. It cheered Melissa.

'As well as can be expected, I think.'

Vivienne knew exactly what she meant. 'I'll see you later, Melly,' she said, going through to her office.

She and Benedict remained locked in discussion until it was time to go home. Melissa popped her head round the door and said goodnight, and Vivienne looked at her watch and said, 'Good lord, is it that time already? Wait for me, Melly, I'm coming.'

On the way home Vivienne said, 'Beebee tells me you're not well. Something about you almost fainting at the office? What happened?'

Melissa grimaced. 'Lack of food, actually. Didn't he tell you?'

Vivienne shook her head.

Typical, thought Melissa, when it was partly his fault. 'I'm all right again now.'

'Good,' said Vivienne, 'because I'm having a dinner party tonight. I've invited Meredith Duncan—you don't know him, but he's both a client and a good friend of mine. And I've asked Beebee to make up a foursome. I'm quite looking forward to it.'

Melissa was horrified. It was clear what Vivienne was doing. 'Oh, Aunt Viv, how could you? You know I'm off men. I don't want anything to do with him, or any man, come to that. I've finished with that sort of thing—for a long time, anyway.'

Vivienne shook her head in disagreement. 'Tim took

you too much for granted. He forgot how to treat you—if he ever knew,' she added disparagingly. 'You never looked like a girl in love. I never liked the boy, and I would have told you so if your mother hadn't stopped me. You're better off without him, Melly.'

Melissa grimaced. 'I know, I've accepted that, but I'm not ready for anyone else. I can't trust anyone now. Tim was so stable, I thought. I never dreamt he'd do this to me. So, please, Aunt Viv, don't try and push me and Benedict together. I've suffered him for three days—and that was enough.'

'Benedict's a gentleman,' said Vivienne quietly. 'He won't force himself on you. But he can be good company, and that's what you need right now. Someone to take you out of yourself, to make you forget Tim, to make you feel like a woman again.'

Melissa smiled weakly. He had done that already. 'For your sake I'll be friendly towards him, but don't expect anything else.'

'As if I would,' laughed Vivienne. 'You're only the two people I care about most in this world.'

In deference to Vivienne, Melissa wore a pretty blue dress for the dinner party. It suited her colouring, and although quite loose-fitting it had a way of outlining her curves without accentuating them too much. But she still refused to wear her hair loose, piling it on top of her head and fixing it in position with two glittering combs. She wore a touch of mascara, but that was all. Her cheeks were flushed anyway and she rarely wore lipstick.

It was a game she was playing now, a game with Benedict. She knew that if she dared to dress up too much he would think she was doing it to impress him and no way did she want him to think that. She did not want him to pay her any more attention.

Meredith Duncan turned out to be a handsome, grey-haired gentleman about Vivienne's own age. He was obviously very much in love with her, but she was oblivious, entirely happy as a single woman, a career woman.

She had apparently done several television commericals for Meredith, and he was an old friend of Benedict's as well. Actually both men adored Vivienne, and why not? She was beautiful still.

'So you are Vivienne's new assistant?' Meredith eyed Melissa as the introductions were made, but his interest remained for no longer than a few seconds. His attention was soon back on the older woman.

This meant that Benedict was able to devote the whole of his time to her, much to Melissa's disgust. 'You're improving,' he announced with a satisfied smile, his eyes of the soft blue material caressing her breasts.

She eyed him crossly. 'Don't think it's for your benefit.'

'Would I be so conceited?' he grinned. He looked superbly handsome in a dark lounge suit and a white silk shirt, and Melissa could not ignore his powerful sexuality.

As the evening progressed she discovered that she was having to fight an attraction for him, despite the fact that he never said a word out of place. It frightened her because she never wanted to let herself get involved again. What was it about this man, she wondered, that was getting through to her so quickly?

When he suggested they take a walk in the garden her

eyes filled with terror. But Vivienne, who had heard the invitation, said at once, 'What a good idea. A breath of fresh air will do you good, Melly, love. It will help you sleep.' And her decision was made for her.

Benedict took her elbow and led her from the room and Melissa's whole body was on fire. He had set himself out to be tender and considerate tonight. He had not laid a finger on her and yet his eyes had seduced her, made love to her; now her whole body was attuned to his.

She wondered at the change in her so soon. Whoever would have guessed that four short weeks after Tim finished with her she would feel like this about another man? It was insanity. She must ignore it; she must do her best to push all such thoughts from her mind.

They strolled side by side down the length of the garden. It was still and peaceful and an almost full moon silvered everything it touched. 'Is something on your mind?' he asked, looking at the grimness on her face.

She shrugged.

'Some man perhaps? The one who caused your unhappiness? Is he the reason you asked Vivienne for a job? I think you ought to tell me about him.'

She frowned. 'Why? What's it to do with you?'

'He's ruining your life.'

'He's ruined my life,' she snapped abruptly.

His brows rose. 'It's that bad? You have no intention of forgetting him? You're parading about in a whole host of unattractive clothes so that no other man will get near you. Is that it?'

Melissa nodded emphatically. 'I've finished with men. There's not one of them can be trusted.'

He looked surprised. 'Because one man let you down

you condemn the whole race?'

'My father walked out on my mother. My sister's husband walked out on her. And then Tim walked out on me. What do you expect me to think? God, I hate you men, every single one of you. All you want is a good time. A bit of living and loving and then it's on to the next girl. I wish someone would tell me what motivates you.'

'I would say,' he said slowly, 'that these men never fully loved their women in the first place.'

'I suppose you would never let your chosen woman down?' she asked scathingly. 'You would never tell a girl you loved her and ask her to marry you, and then change your mind?'

'If I wasn't sure of my love for a woman I would never ask her to marry me,' he said firmly. 'But once I was married, it would be for life. Is that what happened, your fiancé jilted you?'

Melissa nodded faintly, her lips compressed.

'Don't you think you should be congratulating yourself, instead of feeling sorry? In my opinion it was a near miss. He might have waited until after you were married to change his mind.'

'I realise that,' snapped Melissa, 'but that doesn't help how I feel. Have you any idea how long I had been going out with him?'

'None at all.'

'The first time Tim asked me to marry him we were at kindergarten together. The second time was on my eighteenth birthday. He was my next-door neighbour. There was never anyone else for either of us.'

His brows rose. 'That's your mistake. If you had gone out with other boys and then gone back to Tim, I would understand your disappointment; you would have known what you were losing. And if Tim had dated other girls and then decided it was you he wanted, then all would have been well. It's my opinion that your Tim has suddenly realised what he's been missing all these years. Maybe if you wait long enough he'll come back to you. On the other hand, maybe you would not want him back?'

'Never!' spat Melissa angrily. 'Do you know when he actually told me he couldn't go through with it? On our wedding eve. About eighteen hours before the big event. Can you imagine what that did to me?'

He nodded seriously. 'Yes, I think so. How old are you, Melissa?'

She wondered what that had got to do with it. 'Twenty-three.'

'So you were engaged for five whole years? Dammit, if the man loved you he'd never have waited that long. Unless of course he was getting what he wanted?'

'You swine!' Melissa's green eyes flashed sudden fire. 'There was nothing like that between us.'

But she had wondered why Tim had never been interested in the sexual side of their relationship. He had kissed her, often, and they had indulged in light petting, but he had never wanted anything more. She had consoled herself with the thought that he was waiting until they were married. In fact she had congratulated herself on having a man who was considerate enough not to want to hop into bed. It was the in-thing with all her friends, but it had never worried her.

He was watching her closely. 'Doesn't that tell you anything? It's my guess the man never loved you. If he did he would never have been able to keep his hands off you. Nor you him. Did he turn your limbs to fire when he came near? Did you melt when he held you in his arms? I think he took you very much for granted, Melissa. I don't think he knew how to treat you. In fact, I think you respond more to me than you ever did to him.'

Melissa gasped. What a nerve! What a conceit!

'You don't think it's true?' A smile tugged at the corners of his mouth.

'How can it be true?' she demanded. 'You've never even kissed me.'

'A man doesn't have to kiss a woman to sense her response.'

It was a fact; she did feel something. But surely she had given no outward signs?

He moved closer towards her. 'You're very beautiful, Melissa, and it's criminal that you're hiding your true self away.'

Melissa's heart thumped and she could feel the blood pulsing through her veins. She backed a step and put up her hands as if to fend off an attacker.

'Don't be afraid,' he said softly. 'I won't touch you if you don't want me to. All I want to do is help.'

'You can help me by getting out of here now. I don't need your help. I have no intention of ever getting involved with another man.'

'What a waste.' He suddenly caught her hands in his, lifting them to his mouth and pressing kisses into her palms.

Melissa grew hot. He was right. She did respond to him in a way she never had to Tim. This was a totally new experience. She tried to pull away but his grip tightened. She lowered her eyes but he said, 'Look at me.'

She obeyed, and every nerve-end tingled with anticipation. He let her go and lifted his hands to her face, cupping it between his palms, pressing a kiss gently to her brow.

'What excuse did he give you, Melissa, for not wanting to marry you?' he asked softly.

She swallowed and said huskily, 'He said he wasn't—ready, for such a commitment.' Even to her own ears the excuse sounded feeble.

'The bastard!' swore Benedict explosively. 'When would he be ready? What a waste of a beautiful life. I suppose you still saw him every day? You could hardly avoid him. You did the right thing, Melissa, moving away.'

But she wasn't doing the right thing letting him get through to her. There was no way she was ever going to trust any man again.

His fingers were unplaiting her hair now, releasing it from its bondage, arranging it about her face and shoulders. She stood it for as long as she could.

'I think I'd like to go in now,' she said huskily.

He lifted a handful of hair to his face, burying his nose in the silky scented tresses. 'I think we ought to stay here a while longer.''

'I don't think so,' she said.

'Because I'm disturbing you? Because you're afraid of your own feelings?' He put a finger beneath her chin and forced her to look at him.

Melissa met the smoky gaze and felt a tremor run through her. This was madness. Sheer madness. 'What a conceit you have, Mr Burton. I feel nothing for you, nothing at all.

He grinned. 'What a liar you are, Miss Sutherland. Unlike your Tim, I've been out with many girls, and I've learned to read the signals they send out. You'll never convince me that you're immune. But have it your way—for now.'

He let go of her hair but his eyes continued to search her face and Melissa found she could not move. Her heart thumped loudly; she could not recall ever being affected like this before. Please go away, she willed silently. Please.

But her plea was in vain. It was the same as earlier in the evening. He was not touching her, yet he was making love to her. It was as if invisible electric wires ran from his body to hers, and although the voltage was low it was sufficient to send tingles through each and every nerve.

If he was not going to break this spell that bound them, then she would have to do it herself. It was crazy, insane, idiotic. With an effort she twisted free and ran towards the house. 'Goodnight, Benedict.'

He followed, catching her up at the door. 'Goodnight, Melissa. Sleep well.' Then he grinned. 'Call out if you need me.'

'I won't,' she said emphatically. 'And you'd better make sure that door's locked.'

When she got up to her room Melissa shut the door and, leaning back against it, closed her eyes, letting out a deep, unhappy sigh. What was happening to her? For heaven's sake, why was she behaving like this?

She eventually undressed and climbed into bed, but it was a long time before she dropped off to sleep. She was thankful that the nightmare did not return, but she did dream about Benedict—Benedict kissing her, Benedict making love to her, Benedict her constant companion—and she woke feeling completely drained.

Taking one look at her over the breakfast table the next morning, Vivienne said firmly, 'No work for you today, my girl. You look awful. I don't think it was such a good idea after all, you stopping up for my dinner party last night.'

'I had trouble getting to sleep,' protested Melissa, 'but I'm not ill, really I'm not. What would I do with myself all day? I can't stay here. I won't.'

But Vivienne was adamant. 'You look to me as though you need plenty of rest and fresh air. Go for a walk. Sit in the garden. Goodness me, Melly, make the most of it while you can. Once you're fighting fit I'll work you like a horse—and then you'll be begging for a day off.'

Melissa smiled ruefully. 'But all your work——'

'I'll get one of the girls out of the typing pool to do it,' interjected the older woman quickly. 'Don't worry about a thing, Melly. My mind's made up and you should know me well enough to realise that I never change it.'

And no matter how much Melissa protested, Vivienne remained firm.

Melissa sat on at the table long after Vivienne had gone. To be truthful, a day doing absolutely nothing sounded like heaven, though she would never have admitted it. She had pushed herself really hard since Tim had jilted her and it was beginning to tell. She felt absolutely weary, drained both physically and mentally.

When a tap came on the kitchen door Melissa was absolutely amazed to see Benedict.

'What are you doing here? Why aren't you at the office?'

'Now there's a greeting,' he said. 'Viv phoned up and told me she'd given you the day off, and as I'm long overdue some time off myself, I thought I might join you.'

Melissa glared. 'I don't need your company.'

'I must admit you don't look too good,' he said, ignoring her protest and making his way into the kitchen. 'A sleepless night, was it?' He grinned wickedly. 'What are you going to do with yourself?'

She shrugged. 'I haven't the slightest idea.'

'I could take you out for the day.'

Her heart banged painfully. 'Vivienne said I was to rest.'

'You'd be resting in my car.'

'I don't think I want to.'

He eyed her for a moment. 'Afraid, Melissa?'

'No,' she said quickly. 'What is there to be afraid of?' But she was, desperately. She did not want to get involved with Benedict. He was so attractive, so masculine, so sexually exciting. She didn't want to let herself get close.

'Then you have no argument.' His tone was firm. 'If you've finished eating, run along and get ready.'

CHAPTER FOUR

BENEDICT took Melissa to the zoo. The last time she had been there was shortly after her parents' divorce. Tim had gone with them, too, she remembered. He had been a part of her life for so long that it was impossible to recall memories in which he played no part.

'Enjoying it?' Benedict watched her with pleasure as she laughed when one of the monkeys crept up behind another and stole the rope he was busily trying to fasten round a piece of wood.

She nodded, her eyes shining, unconscious of how beautiful she looked. She wore a pale blue pleated skirt and a deeper blue cotton top, and she had tied her hair with a blue scarf in her nape. She had mascaraed her lashes and applied faint blue shadow, and her cheeks were flushed with the warmth of the sun. He thought she looked happier than she had since he'd met her.

'Are you ready to move on?'

'If you like.'

'Or we can stay here a bit longer?'

How considerate he was this afternoon. Why hadn't he been like this in the beginning? Why had he shown her the other side to his character, a side she did not like, a side which had immediately put her on the defensive?

'I'd love to see the sea-lions,' she said.

The zoo was crowded with schoolchildren and he took

her arm. Melissa felt the now familiar thrill and was actually disappointed when he let her go once they were free of the crowd.

They wandered from enclosure to enclosure, admiring and exclaiming, laughing and sighing. Benedict was friendly and entertaining. He only touched her when it was necessary—and she grew more aware of him with every minute that passed.

After their tour of the zoo they ate lunch in a crowded pub, balancing their plates on their knees, and Melissa realised with amazement how happy she was. She had been so afraid he would push himself on her, but he had done nothing of the sort. He was a good companion—just as Tim had been!

The thought jolted her. Was that all Tim had wanted from her—companionship? Was that why he had never demanded a deeper relationship?

'What's wrong?'

Melissa looked up to find Benedict gazing frowningly at her.

'Nothing. Why?'

'What were you thinking?'

She grimaced self-consciously. 'Actually, about Tim.'

Benedict's mouth thinned. 'And what made him come into your mind right now?'

He sounded jealous! Was that possible? No, it must be her imagination.

'I was——' Dare she say she was comparing the two of them? 'I was——'

'Wishing I were he?' he demanded angrily when she hesitated yet again.

'No, no, nothing like that,' she protested. 'As a matter

of fact I was thinking that perhaps all Tim ever wanted from me was companionship. He was an only child, you see. His mother couldn't have any more. I think that's why he was always round at our house.'

'That sounds a very logical conclusion. I wonder why you didn't see it before?'

Melissa pulled a face. 'I suppose I'm looking at him in a different light now.'

'You're not still hankering after him?' he demanded fiercely.

She shook her head.

'Because he's not worth it.'

'I know.'

He lifted her plate off her lap and caught her hands between his own. They dwarfed hers, big and brown and strong, and unwanted feelings raced through her, feelings that had been building up all day. She pulled away. 'What are we going to do now?'

She missed his frown, saw only the heart-stopping smile. How handsome he was.

'How about an afternoon on the river?'

She clapped her hands delightedly. 'Lovely. I went with Tim once and——' She stopped immediately, clapping her hands to her mouth. 'I'm sorry.'

He sighed heavily. 'I realise it can't be easy remembering he's no longer a part of your life, but I'd prefer not to be reminded of him at every turn. I don't think the river's a good idea after all.'

'Oh, but I want to,' protested Melissa. 'Really I do. I won't mention Tim again, honestly.'

And so he hired a rowing-boat and she sat back in her seat and watched him. He made it look effortless, although she knew it wasn't. he took off his shirt after a few minutes and she admired his hard muscles beneath the darkly tanned skin.

As it was mid-week, there were not many boats on the river and it was peaceful and beautiful. There were moorhens and mallards, dragonflies and kingfishers, and a heron, and blue, blue skies—and a rare contentment within her.

Constantly her eyes shifted from the passing scenery to Benedict's hard, flat, toned body. There was not one ounce of superfluous fat on him. 'How do you keep so fit?'

He grinned. 'Rowing pretty girls down the river.'

'No, seriously?'

'Jogging every morning, a work-out with weights.'

'How do you find time?'

'I'm an early riser.'

'I'm very impressed. You make me feel decidedly lazy.'

'Why not come jogging with me?'

'I don't think so,' she demurred.

'Coward.'

'I'm not the sporty type.'

'Then you should be. A healthy body is a healthy mind, isn't that what they say? Who knows, a bit of physical exercise might help you forget Tim.'

'You mentioned him, not me,' pointed out Melissa with a smile.

He nodded ruefully. 'He has a strange habit of intruding into the conversation. I think it's about time we turned back.'

'Oh, no!' Melissa's cry was involuntary.

'You're enjoying it?'

She nodded

'Aha,' he grinned. 'I'm making progress at last.'

The sun beat down on them and Melissa felt so comfortable she did not want the day to end. It was with regret that she finally climbed out of the boat.

And then suddenly it rained. A fleeting shower, but sharp and drenching, and they raced for his car. When they got inside he forgot himself and, leaning across, he took her into his arms and kissed her.

It was actually quite a gentle kiss but Melissa had been attuned to him all day and it set off a violent reaction inside her. Her adrenalin level shot up and her heart raced, and for just a second she was enjoying it.

Then she remembered her vows and she pushed against him with all her strength, so hard that he rocked back against the steering wheel, and his eyes narrowed. 'What the devil did you do that for?'

'Because I don't want you to kiss me.'

'Hell, you're not still hung up, are you? I thought we'd actually got somewhere today.'

'I enjoyed your company, yes,' admitted Melissa heavily, 'but I have no intention of getting involved.' She did not want to get close to any man again. It would make her too vulnerable, leave her wide open for more hurt.

'Since when has a kiss constituted a love affair?' he growled, rubbing his side with his hand.

'It has to start somewhere.'

'And you think that's what I'm after?' His eyes were narrowed and watchful.

She swallowed and shrugged. 'I don't know. Isn't it what all men want?'

'Not all men, Melissa,' he rasped. 'And from what

you say, Tim didn't want it either. Was that why you clung to him all those years, someone safe and dependable, someone who wouldn't make any demands on you? Was it you who was to blame? Are you afraid of sex, Melissa? Is that the real truth of the matter?'

'Of course not! How dare you!' Melissa eyed him furiously.

'Then prove it.' His gaze never left her face as he moved again towards her. 'Kiss me, Melissa. Show me that you're not afraid.'

Her heart thudded and for an insane moment she wanted nothing more than to be held against his hard firm body, to feel his lips on hers, to taste him, to experience him, to wallow in excitement such as Tim had never been able to give her. But why should she? Why should she give in? She wasn't afraid, it was just that she didn't want to kiss him; she didn't want that sort of a relationship.

She eased herself back against the door. 'Get away, Benedict. I've not changed my mind, nor will I. Just leave me alone.'

He eyed her savagely for a long moment and then with a snarl he started the engine and the black monster leaped forward, throwing her violently back in her seat. 'If you ask me, Melissa, you're heading the right way to a lifetime of loneliness.'

'How do you make that out?' She snapped her seatbelt into position and sat rigid. 'There's no man in Vivienne's life and it doesn't worry her.'

'Vivienne's in love with her work. Any man interested in Viv would have to come second-best.'

'There's no reason why I shouldn't make my career my life.'

His brows rose. 'You haven't Vivienne's drive.'

'And how would you know?' she demanded.

'I regard myself as a pretty good judge of character.'

'And you've decided that I've no ambition, that I'm sexless, that I——'

He held his hand up to stop her. 'I didn't say you were sexless, Melissa. Far from it. I won't tell you what it does to me just looking at you.' He paused a moment and smiled at his thoughts. 'What I did say was that you were scared of sex. Isn't that right?'

'No!' she said firmly. 'I'll tell you what I'm scared of. I'm scared of getting involved again. I don't want any more commitments. I'm afraid to trust.'

He sighed heavily. 'You're out of your mind. How the hell are you going to learn to trust anyone if you don't give yourself a chance?'

'I will—one day,' she said. 'It's too soon yet. Everything's so raw and new and——'

'And how long do you propose waiting?' he demanded scornfully. 'Till you're too old? Till you lose all the chances you're ever likely to get?' His tone changed, grew softer, more persuasive. 'You're a very beautiful girl, Melissa. Don't try to hide it. Whatever you do don't hide it. Things won't always look this black. You won't always view men with suspicion.' He was silent for a moment, then he said, angrily again, 'Why did we have to meet now, while you're like this? Why won't you let me help? Melissa, I can help you, I know I can.'

'No!' She shook her head, her eyes closed, dismissing him. 'No, Benedict. *No.*' Yet how she was tempted . . .

He swore beneath his breath and neither of them spoke for the rest of the journey. When they got home

Melissa went straight to her room, not even going down for dinner.

'Melly, what's wrong?' Vivienne came to find her. 'I saw Beebee with a face like thunder. He says you went out together; now you're refusing to eat. What happened?'

She eyed the older woman, her mouth twisted wryly. 'Let's say we didn't quite see eye to eye. It was my fault, I should never have gone.'

'What did you fall out over?' Vivienne sounded puzzled.

'Let's say he wanted more than I was prepared to give.'

An eyebrow rose knowingly. 'And he didn't take your rejection kindly?'

Melissa shook her head.

'Beebee's not used to girls saying no,' said Vivienne with an amused smile.

'It wasn't just that,' confessed Melissa. 'He thinks I've got a hang-up, about Tim, about sex, about men in general.'

'And haven't you?' enquired Vivienne archly.

Melissa shrugged. 'Maybe I have, maybe I haven't. Why can't people leave me alone? Why can't I be allowed to get on with my life the way I want to?' Her voice rose shrilly and Vivienne laid a calming hand on her shoulder.

'We want to help, Melly, love, that's all. Are you sure you don't want anything to eat? You're not going to get better like this.'

But Melissa was adamant.

The following morning Melissa was determined to go to work. Staying at home had proved disastrous. Vivienne looked at her closely across the breakfast table, observing the shadows beneath the girl's eyes, the pallor of her skin, and the way her hair was still scraped unbecomingly back, and she shook her head.

'If you won't help yourself, Melly, then I'm going to have to take charge. Your mother phoned last night. You were asleep,' she added quickly when Melissa's head jerked. 'She was naturally disturbed when I told her there wasn't much improvement.'

'I've been gone less than a week,' protested Melissa. 'What does she expect, a miracle?'

'None of us expects miracles,' said Vivienne softly. 'But we do expect you to begin facing the world again.'

'Why haven't you ever married, Aunt Viv?' asked Melissa abruptly.

'Not because I didn't have the opportunity,' said Vivienne sharply. 'But I put my career first and before I knew it it was too late. I lost the only man I ever loved.'

'Meredith seems interested.'

Vivienne shook her head and laughed. 'Meredith is a charmer, he's been after me for years. But I don't love him, and he knows it. And don't try to change the subject, my girl. What I want you to do after breakfast is put your best dress on and paint your face, and then you're coming with me to see one of my most important clients.'

There was a glint in Vivienne's eyes that made Melissa suspicious. 'Who?'

'Clifford Drew.'

'Of Drew & Company, the jewellers?'

Vivienne nodded. 'You've already met Bob Hennessy, I believe? He'll be at the meeting, too. But it's Clifford I want you to met. He'll do your morale good if nothing else. He's a charmer. So make the most of yourself,

Melly. Don't drag your hair back in that hideous fashion, flaunt it. Do it for my company image if not for yourself.'

Melissa attempted to refuse but Vivienne would have none of it, and when she finally presented herself downstairs for Vivienne's inspection the woman was well pleased.

'Perfect! I can't wait to see Clifford's face.'

Melissa groaned. She did not think she wanted to meet this Clifford guy. He sounded like a woman-eater—a bit like Benedict. The sort she desperately wanted to avoid.

'Mint green is your colour without a doubt,' enthused Vivienne, 'and that bag and those shoes, where on earth did you get them?' They were a shiny conker colour that exactly matched her hair.

'This was supposed to be my going-away outfit,' admitted Melissa, picking a hair off the shoulder of her jacket.

'Oh,' said the older woman, nonplussed for a second. Then, 'Ah, well, it's come in useful after all.'

Clifford Drew was roughly Benedict's age, though his hair was already noticeably greying. He was tall, he had a craggy, interesting sort of face, and a deep, deep voice. She went into his office prepared to hate him, and within seconds had fallen under his spell. He had a keen sense of humour, an infectious smile, and the kindest blue eyes Melissa had ever seen. He treated her the same as he did Vivienne, with respect, with courtesy and with friendliness.

'So you are Vivienne's new assistant?' His grip was firm and warm. He flashed a glance at Bob Hennessy, who stood a few paces behind him. 'You'd better make an appointment at the opticians.'

Bob caught Melissa's eye and looked faintly uncomfortable, but she grinned consolingly; the change in her must have been quite a shock for him. Although she would have liked to know what it was he had said.

The meeting started, Vivienne trying to push her campaign, Bob still opting for an update of the old commercial, Clifford listening and commenting and nodding, but mostly watching Melissa.

The funny thing was, he did not make her feel uncomfortable. There was nothing suggestive in his gaze. She appealed to him aesthetically. His whole office reflected his love of beauty: the little carved ornaments, the beautifully framed prints, the soft, deep, heather-coloured carpet, the antique desk, the silver inkwell.

She smiled when their eyes met, which was frequently, but for most of the time she listened attentively to the conversation revolving around her.

'Well, Melissa—or may I call you Melly?' smiled Clifford. 'You've heard the suggestions. Which one do you think we ought to use?'

Melissa had not realised she would be expected to make any structural comments, but his smile was so encouraging that she spoke almost without thinking.

'Actually, I have an idea of my own.'

She caught Vivienne's surprise out of the corner of her eye, saw Clifford Drew's dark brows rise, and was aware of Bob Hennessy sitting that little bit straighter.

'I did try to tell Benedict, but he wouldn't listen. Actually I don't know whether it's acceptable, or even whether it's been done before, but——'

'We'll soon tell you that,' cut in Vivienne.

Clifford raised his hand. 'Let the girl speak.' He

smiled at Melissa encouragingly.

Melissa closed her eyes in order to see the image more clearly. 'I have this vision of a man lying down, on the beach perhaps; he's tough and masculine and sexy, his skin and the hairs on his chest are wet after his swim, the drops of water glistening in the sunlight.'

Or were they tears? A sudden image of Benedict floated before her mind's eye. She opened her eyes and looked at her audience. They were watching her closely.

'But shining more brightly are the diamonds lying across his chest. A woman's hand, her fingers long, her nails polished, slides inch by sensual inch over his body, loving him, searching, feeling, finally finding her prize. She picks it up, maybe a necklace, or earrings, and holds it reverently in the palm of her hand. This is for her? The question is plain on her face. The man smiles and nods. A beautiful gift for a beautiful woman.'

She blushed furiously when she had finished. It had been Benedict's body, her hand. Oh, God, she hoped they hadn't guessed. 'Something like that,' she said, trying to laugh. 'Unless you think it's too foolish?'

'Foolish? It's brilliant.' Clifford stood up and took her hands in his. 'You're an angel. You're a credit to Vivienne. A few more ideas like that and she'll be so successful I won't be able to pay her fees.'

Vivienne was smiling, too, though a faint frown creased her brow. 'Why did you keep the idea to yourself, Melly? It's fantastic. You say Beebee wouldn't listen?'

'Not when I first tried to voice my opinion. But I must admit I didn't actually tell him about this particular idea. I thought it was pretty stupid.' She looked at the faces around her. 'Well, I did. I've never thought up a commercial before, and most of them these days are pretty hard-hitting.'

'Yes, but Christmas is different,' said Clifford. 'It's the men we have to seduce at this time of year. And what man wouldn't imagine himself in that sort of situation? I bet there'll be a few naked bodies on Christmas morning. Who do you think we should have for our man?'

Melissa felt her colour rise again. Viv's eyes were upon her. She knew!

She attempted to laugh. 'I've really no idea. Any man with a good body would do.'

The idea was discussed in greater detail. They drank coffee and talked some more. Then Bob Hennesy went back to his office and Clifford asked Melissa if he could take her out to dinner.

'It's the least I can do,' he added pleadingly.

Melissa was about to refuse when she saw Vivienne discreetly nodding her head. And after an inner battle with herself she gave in.

'Thank you, I'd like that.' And the surprising thing was that she really meant it.

CHAPTER FIVE

MELISSA dressed with care for her date with Clifford, yet it was with Benedict that her thoughts lay. For the thousandth time she asked herself why she had rejected him when all the time her body had been responding?

Why hadn't she let him kiss her? Why hadn't she given herself the pleasure of feeling his arms around her, his mouth on hers? There was a whole world of difference between his touch and Tim's. Tim had never excited her. Their's had been a comfortable relationship, built up over the years. This was something new and exhilarating.

Was Benedict right when he said she was afraid of sex? Admittedly the intense desire she felt did frighten her. It did not seem possible that she could experience such feelings on so short an acquaintance. But to be actually afraid of him touching her, of responding, of enjoying a physical relationship—that was nonsense. She wasn't afraid. Wary perhaps; he was an unknown quantity. he was pushing her too quickly, too soon.

She smoothed her dress over her hips and wondered what Benedict would think of her now. Her hair hung half-way down her back in deep, rich waves, her eyes were enhanced with copper eyeshadow, her lashes lengthened with mascara. She had applied blusher to her cheeks and wore a dull red lipstick.

Her dress was silk, in copper and beige, high at the

front, scooped daringly low at the back. A gold chain belt emphasised her tiny waist and the skirt fell in soft unpressed pleats. Her high-heeled sandals were beige, as too was the tiny evening bag with its gilt chainstrap. She fixed gold pendant earrings in her ears and fastened a gold chain about her neck, and was ready.

She gave herself one final check in the mirror, listening to the skirt rustle as she twirled this way and that. A smile lifted her lips and her eyes held a sparkle of anticipation. She tried to convince herself that it was for Clifford, but she could not help pretending that she was showing herself off to Benedict. She could imagine the surprise in his eyes, the admiration, the desire! This was how he had wanted to see her.

When she went downstairs Clifford was waiting. Melissa was surprised because she had not heard him come. Both he and Vivienne looked up when she entered the room, Vivienne smiled and nodding approvingly, Clifford grinning like a Cheshire cat, holding out both hands for hers, unashamedly eyeing her up and down.

'Hello, Clifford,' she said shyly.

'Melly, what can I say? You're exquisite, perfect. What a lot of attention we'll attract tonight. Beauty and the Beast, no less.'

'You're no beast,' she laughingly protested. In fact he looked pretty good himself in a grey pin-striped suit and a white shirt. With his prematurely greying hair he looked very distinguished and handsome.

He offered her his arm and she took it, and he inclined his head towards Vivienne. 'I'll take very good care of her.'

'I know you will,' said Vivienne. 'Have a good time,

both of you.'

The restaurant was exclusive and intimate, the food superb, and Clifford excellent company. He was attentive without being overpowering. He flattered her, yet there were no sexual undertones to anything he said. He was a perfect companion, reducing her to fits of laughter with some of the tales he had to tell, keeping her entertained the whole evening through.

She learned that he had lost his wife several years ago and had no intention of getting married again. 'But I'm not averse to female company,' he grinned.

'You sound just my type,' she said, and proceeded to tell him about Tim. 'It's left me very distrustful. I don't mind telling you that I have no intention of getting married, either.'

His brows rose. 'You're far too young and pretty to make such sweeping statements. All you need is time; it's a great healer. And then one day you'll meet the right man—and what a lucky guy he will be.'

'You wouldn't like to lay a bet on that, would you?' she quipped.

'I couldn't take your money off you,' he chuckled.

They talked and talked and the time fled; Melissa was staggered when he said they must leave.

At Vivienne's door he gravely took her hand. 'Goodnight, my princess. Thank you for a lovely evening. I'd like to see you again, if I may? If I don't bore you too much?'

Melissa smiled. 'Clifford, you could never bore me. I've enjoyed myself very much. And yes, please, I would like to go out with you again.' He did her so much good. There were no pressures, just sheer, unadulterated, relaxing pleasure.

When she went to bed Melissa could not help thinking about Benedict on the floor above her. Had he seen her going out with Clifford? Had he observed her coming back? If so, what was he thinking? Was he jealous? And although she had had a marvellous time, Melissa knew that deep down in her heart she would have preferred Benedict's company. He had got through to her whether she wanted it or not.

All the next day at the office Melissa waited for Benedict to walk in, but there was no sign of him. He was either keeping himself very much to himself, or he was out on business. She could have asked Vivienne, but that would have given herself away.

When she got home an enormous bouquet of flowers was awaiting her. They were gorgeous: cream roses, yellow lilies, white carnations. Beautiful. She buried her nose in them, inhaling their fragrance, and then searched for the card. But there was nothing.

So who had sent them? Clifford? Benedict? She knew who she wanted them to be from. But when Clifford phoned her later she knew her wish had not come true.

In the weeks that followed he showered her with trinkets and flowers and at all times remained a perfect gentleman. He was content with just her company; he asked for nothing more. And he did her good. He made her forget her problems. She dressed up for him and the colour returned to her cheeks, and she looked once again the beautiful girl she had been before Tim jilted her.

She saw nothing of Benedict. He was out of the office a lot, and he never came to see Vivienne, she always went to him. It was clear he was avoiding her, and Melissa could not explain how hurt she felt.

Then one day her office door opened and he walked in. Melissa's heart flipped. How good he looked. How handsome. How sexy! And how she had missed him. She wanted to run across the room and throw herself into his arms. But the circumstances under which they had parted made that impossible. In fact he would have been deeply shocked if he could have read her thoughts.

For several moments he stood looking at her, at her hair hanging loose the way he liked it, at her wide eyes, her lids brushed with green shadow, her glossy lips parted expectantly. At the frilly blouse and the skirt which outlined her trim figure. She no longer felt any need to hide behind shapeless clothes. Benedict had begun to give her her confidence back, Clifford had finished the job.

'You're looking good, Melissa.'

She nodded. 'I don't think of Tim much these days.' And that was the truth, she realised with surprise. When she wasn't with Clifford it was Benedict who filled her mind. And now he was here, looking at her as though she was someone special, and her pulses throbbed and her heart wouldn't stop racing.

'I guess I rushed you,' he said, moving further into the room.

She said nothing, just stood there looking at him. He was so handsome. So tall and strong.

'Melissa, I——' He stopped and changed his mind. 'Will you have dinner with me tonight?'

'Oh, Benedict, I'm sorry, but I've already arranged to go out.' She hated saying this to him; her heart was pounding and she wanted more than anything to spend some time with him.

'With Viv? I'm sure she won't mind when she——'

'No, not with Viv,' cut in Melissa quickly.

He frowned. 'Another man?'

Melissa nodded, biting her bottom lip when she saw the sudden anger on his face.

'Dammit, Melissa, what's happened to your aversion to men? It was mighty short-lived. Or was it simply me you were against? Who is he? Who the hell is he? Is he the reason for this—this transformation?'

It was no good trying to pretend she did not know what he meant. 'It's Clifford Drew,' she said quietly.

'Clifford Drew?' His eyes shot wide. 'Clifford Drew of Drew's the jewellers?'

She nodded.

'He's a widower.'

'Yes, I know. What difference does that make?'

'He's too old for you.'

'He's not much older than you. Heavens, Benedict, we're just friends, that's all.'

'You're forgetting I know Clifford. He's not likely to settle for——'

He stopped abruptly when the phone rang and Melissa picked it up, but his eyes glared and she could see his fingers curling into his palms.

'Melly, my princess, how are you?'

Unbidden swift colour flooded her cheeks. 'I'm fine, and how are you? How's your cold?'

'I'm keeping it at bay with that homeopathic remedy you recommended. I'm just confirming tonight—in case you were wondering whether I'd be fit enough. It will take more than a few sneezes to knock me off my feet.'

Melissa smiled. 'I know that, Clifford.'

Benedict's face turned red when he heard her mention the other man's name, and he would have snatched the phone if she hadn't held it away from him.

'Yes, Clifford, I'm still here. I have someone in my office—but he's just going.' She glared pointedly at Benedict.

Savagely he swung on his heel and crashed through into Vivienne's office.

She spent a few more minutes talking to Clifford and then attempted to finish the letter in her typewriter. But it was a sheer impossibility. How could she concentrate while Benedict was in there? How could she ignore him? He was larger than life. And she thought she was a little in love with him!

In love? It was crazy—yet for what other reason had her stomach turned upside down when he walked into the room? Why had her mouth gone dry? Why did her loins ache? Why had she missed him so much? But it was not love; it could not be. She wouldn't let it be. It was simply a chemical attraction, nothing more. She took a deep breath and closed her eyes, and when she opened them again he was standing in front of her.

'I'm sorry, Melissa, I shouldn't have gone on at you like that.' He didn't look sorry. A fierce frown still carved his brow, and his eyes, which could be so sensual, were as hard as polished jet. 'You have your own life to lead and it's no business of mine what you do with it.'

'That's right,' she said tightly, 'it's none of your business.' Wasn't it strange how, when you were hurt, you said things you didn't mean? She wanted Benedict to understand, she wanted to explain that there was nothing in it, that Clifford was a friend and nothing more and that in his way he was helping her overcome her distrust of men.

His lips thinned and he turned and slammed out of the office. A few minutes later Vivienne followed. 'I'll see you at home,' she said cheerfully to Melissa. 'You can sign my letters for me.'

Evidently Benedict had said nothing about Clifford, though quite how he had managed to control himself Melissa was not sure. And how she managed to get through the rest of the day she did not know either.

Benedict's sudden appearance had done her system no good at all. She was glad when it was time to pack up and go home. She had answered telephone queries automatically, and typed Vivienne's letters and signed them with less than half her mind on what she was doing. She just hoped that everything she had said and done this afternoon made sense.

To her dismay she learned that Vivienne had invited Benedict to dinner. 'I thought we might have a nice cosy evening together.'

And then she would go to bed early and there would be just the two of them. Melissa knew exactly the way Vivienne's mind worked. 'I have a date with Clifford.'

'If you don't mind me saying so,' said Vivienne, 'I think you're seeing too much of him. I know I started it all but I never intended you to get this involved.'

'I'm not involved,' answered Melissa. 'We're friends, that's all. There's nothing in it. He'll never get over his wife, if the truth's known. He's always talking about her.'

'Then he surely won't mind if you cancel your date?'

'I don't see why I should,' said Melissa sharply, even though the thought of spending an evening with Benedict

set her pulses racing. Why, oh why, did he have to make
her feel like this?

Clifford was her armour, her defence, and the fact that
he wanted nothing more from her than friendship made
her all the fonder of him. 'If you'll excuse me, Aunt Viv, I
must go and get ready.'

Vivienne looked disappointed but she said no more and
Melissa went slowly up to her room. Slowly because
suddenly she was not looking forward to tonight so much.

Melissa made even more of an effort with her
appearance than usual. Her soft amber-coloured dress, in
a shiny polyester material that looked like satin, was
figure-hugging and sophisticated. It had a straight skirt, a
peplum waist and a wide gold mesh belt. She looked very
elegant in high-heeled gold sandals, with her hair pinned
back at the sides but hanging in heavy burnished chestnut
waves down her back. In her ears were a pair of amber
earrings given to her by Clifford.

Her make-up was discreet but effective and she knew
Clifford would be very proud of her tonight. He always
took her to smart places and it was her pleasure to dress
up for him. But tonight there was another reason why she
wanted to look her best. Not to impress Benedict, she
assured herself, but to show him that she didn't give a
damn what he thought. She enjoyed Clifford's company
and nothing he said would make her stop going out with
him.

When she went downstairs Benedict was in the lounge
with Vivienne. His eyes missed nothing, narrowing and
growing harder by the second. 'Lucky man, Clifford. I
must ask him what his secret is.'

Melissa held her head that much higher. 'Let's say he

knows how to treat a girl.'

'Meaning I don't?'

His tone was harsh and Vivienne glanced anxiously from him to Melissa.

'Clifford's a real gentleman. He makes me feel——' Melissa paused, pretending to search for the right word, experiencing a certain grim pleasure when she saw the increasing anger on Benedict's face. 'He makes me feel cherished, and safe. He's done me so much good—as you can see.'

She twirled around for Benedict to view her from every angle. 'Do you approve?'

He swore loudly as he picked up his glass and tossed back the remainder of his whisky. 'What the hell does my opinion matter to you?'

Vivienne frowned. 'Oh, dear, what's wrong with you two?'

'I don't approve of her seeing Clifford Drew,' snarled Benedict, then he grimaced. 'I'm sorry, Viv. It really has nothing to do with me, has it?'

'I think——' began Vivienne, and then the doorbell rang and Melissa hurried to answer it, conscious of Benedict's gaze stabbing her in the back.

'Melly, my princess, you're more beautiful than ever. I'm honoured indeed.' Clifford took her hand and dramatically lifted it to his lips.

Melissa smiled. 'Come in and say hello. Viv has a guest—someone I think you already know.'

Clifford frowned his curiosity as he followed her into the house and into the room where Vivienne and Benedict sat. Melissa watched Benedict's face closely as Clifford greeted Vivienne, feeling a certain satisfaction when she saw the grimness of his lips and the hostility in his eyes.

But nevertheless Benedict smiled politely as he stood up to shake the other man's hand. 'Clifford, how are you? It's been, how long, since I last saw you? Two years?'

'I guess so.'

'And how's business?'

'Booming, and thanks to Melly here we have a wonderful new ad in the pipeline for the run up to Christmas.' Clifford put his arm round Melissa's shoulders and smiled fondly down into her face. 'She's a wonderful girl, full of great ideas, and incidentally the best thing that's happened to me in a long time.'

Melissa had not expected Clifford to sing her praises there and then, or so highly, and she felt slight unease when she saw Benedict's harsh frown.

'Really?' His tone was absolutely cold and held none of his earlier warmth, forced though that had been.

'Absolutely. I feel like a new man. I mean, just look at her. What man wouldn't be proud to have her on his arm? She does me good.' He smiled indulgently down at Melissa. 'And I have Vivienne to thank for introducing us.' His smile encompassed the older woman, too.

'And she approves, of your—er—friendship?' Benedict managed to make the word sound dirty.

Clifford frowned, but before he could say anything Melissa tugged at his arm. 'I think we should go.' A verbal battle between Benedict and Clifford was the last thing she wanted.

'If you say so, my princess.' Clifford's smile returned. '*Au revoir*, Vivienne. Benedict.' His nod towards the other man was clearly puzzled.

During the short drive to the restaurant Clifford said nothing about Benedict's behaviour, instead relating an amusing incident that had happened to him that day.

He really was a darling, thought Melissa, always doing his best to make her happy. He chased away her slightest frown with his countless anecdotes, and claimed that she, in her turn, had brought a new meaning to his life.

It was not until they were half-way through their main course that he mentioned Benedict. 'He seems not to approve of you seeing me.'

'He doesn't,' agreed Melissa, grimacing ruefully.

'Have you any idea why?'

She shrugged. 'Not really.' How could she tell him?

'Unless he's interested in you himself?'

'I have been out with him a couple of times,' admitted Melissa, wondering why she felt so guilty about admitting this to Clifford.

He looked startled. 'I didn't realise, or I would never have taken up so much of your time.'

'Oh, you're not! No! There's nothing between me and Benedict, honestly.'

Clifford frowned. 'He sounded almost—possessive?'

'We had a row.'

'And now he's jealous that you're seeing me?'

Benedict jealous? That was the last thing he would be. 'I don't know and I don't care,' she said vehemently. 'I think he wants an affair but I'm not into that sort of thing. Let's forget him.'

Clifford eyed her shrewdly and then smiled. 'He's not the only man who's attracted to you.'

Her eyes widened.

'I hadn't meant to say anything, Melissa. I know

you're still nursing a grudge against the whole male race.
But I think now is the time.'

'Clifford?' She frowned slightly.

'You must know I've grown very fond of you. You've
helped me as much as I hope I've helped you. One day I'd
like to think that you'll feel more for me than just
friendship.'

'I don't know,' she whispered.

'The truth is, I've fallen in love with you, Melly.
Something I'd never expected to happen. And something
I didn't mean to tell you, not yet, not for a long time.'

He touched her hand across the table, gently stroking
her skin. 'But I'm a patient man and I shan't mention it
again. You must dictate our future, whether you want to
just remain friends, no strings attached, or whether at
some date you develop an affection for me. It's entirely up
to you. You can even end it all here and now if you
like—if I've upset you, if I've said too much. All I want is
for you to be happy, Melly. That is the most important
thing in my life.

'Clifford, what can I say?' Melissa took his hand
between her own. 'I feel very humble. I don't deserve
you.'

'Nonsense,' he said briskly.

'I don't love you, Clifford, I have to be honest. But I do
value your friendship. And I'd still like to see you. If
that's all right?' She felt strangely close to tears.

'Of course.'

'It's not asking too much?'

'I'm happy just to be with you,' he said. 'And I shall
never give up hoping. But you may rest assured that I
shall never push you. I understand too much what

you've gone through. To me, falling in love with you is a miracle. I never thought I'd love another woman. Who knows? Perhaps one day another miracle will happen.'

'Who knows?' she agreed. But it would not be Clifford who would capture her heart, though goodness knew he deserved it. He was the kindest man she had ever met. And so patient. He deserved better than her.

It was almost midnight when he finally took her home. He held her hand for a brief moment and kissed her, an oh, so gentle kiss that lit no fires, then he waited until she was safely inside before driving away.

He was such a gentlman. He really was the nicest man Melissa had ever met. It was a pity she did not love him. A smile played on her lips as she shot the bolts on the door, only to have it wiped away completely when Benedict's voice sounded harshly behind her.

'About time, too.'

She swung round. 'What are you doing here? Is Vivienne still up?'

His nostrils flared and he looked angry and tired, and she noticed for the first time how much thinner his face was—or was it the hall lighting that cast unflattering shadows?

'Vivienne's gone to bed. I was about to leave when I saw Clifford's car draw up. Any caring man would have had you home long before now. Has he forgotten you have to go to work in the morning?'

She eyed him coolly. 'Are you suggesting that Clifford does not care about me?'

'Clifford probably cares more about himself than you,' he jeered derisively.

'How dare you! Clifford's a darling. He's a perfect gentleman, and my happiness is his main concern.'

'I bet it is,' he retorted crisply, marching through into Vivienne's sitting-room and pouring himself a glass of whisky.

'And what is that supposed to mean?' she demanded, following him and eyeing him savagely. Heavens, what had brought this on? Had he been simmering all evening? What a suspicious mind he had. She could hardly believe what he was insinuating.

'I want to know what's going on between you two,' he rasped, tossing back a mouthful of the fiery liquid.

'I don't suppose you'd believe me if I said "nothing"?' she demanded angrily.

'You're right, I wouldn't. And no one else seeing the transformation in you would believe it either. Take a look at yourself, Melissa. Take a look.'

He clamped her shoulders with powerful fingers and propelled her firmly towards the mirror over the fireplace. Melissa met her own eyes, green and over-bright, her cheeks flushed, her lips soft and parted.

But this wasn't Clifford's doing. Admittedly she had had a very pleasant evening—didn't she always?—and he had dropped quite a bombshell when he had said he loved her, but Benedict was responsible for her expression now. Her heightened colour, her brilliant eyes, they were his fault. It was anger, not passion, that gave her face life.

In the mirror she met his eyes, too. They had darkened to nearly black, and there was an almost fanatical fierceness to them which she failed to understand. 'I don't know why you're so angry.'

'Because, Melissa, I can't accept that you're willing to trust him, and yet you won't trust me. Maybe he hasn't tried anything on yet, though I doubt it.'

'Your despicable,' she scorned. 'Everyone's not like you. Clifford's doing me good, and nothing you say will make any difference. So if you've quite finished perhaps you'd let me go. I'm tired and, as you say, I do have work tomorrow.'

'I'll let you go when I'm good and ready,' he snarled.

He pulled her back hard against him and Melissa felt the urgent thud of his heart—and something else, too: her own heart pounding in unison with his, excitement accelerated along each and every vein.

It was still nothing more than a physical thing, she insisted to herself, closing her eyes so that he should read nothing in them. He was a very sexual man; it would be impossible not to be affected by him, but she did not love him, surely? There was nothing emotional in her response, and so long as she continued to fight the attraction there never would be.

'Melissa, I don't want you to be friends with that man.'

Her eyes shot wide open. 'You can't stop me.'

His hands were sliding down her arms, exploring the softness of her skin, and then they were round her waist, and the next moment he had spun her to face him. 'Melissa, I want——' He stopped and groaned. 'God, Melissa, I want you.'

Before she could stop him his mouth claimed hers. For just a moment there was a desperate hunger in him, his lips bruising and hurting, demanding and taking, while she stood passively to attention. But it was a struggle. She was responding to him in a way she had never imagined possible.

Suddenly Melissa felt the tautness go out of him. His arms held her still, but she could escape if she wanted to. So why didn't she?

His hand came to her chin, tilting it so that he could look into her eyes. She felt as though he were looking deep inside her, that he was reading her mind, that he knew what he could do to her.

Then his hand moved behind her head, holding it so that he could kiss her, his lips moving slowly and sensually over hers, his tongue followed the same path. It was a kiss like no other, inciting, arousing, and her lips parted of their own volition, excitement mounting in her.

But he was not ready yet to plunder the softness of her mouth. His tongue and lips brushed the delicate column of her throat, lingering on the pulse that beat its own tell-tale rhythm, then moving up again to tease the corners of her mouth and the delicate area behind her ears. Shiver after shiver of sheer sensual pleasure rode down Melissa's spine. Tim had never done anything like this. She had not known such sexual excitement existed.

He returned to her mouth, taking her bottom lip into his own, nibbling and sucking, and driving her half crazy. She was not even aware of her moan of pleasure, nor that her hands were reaching for his head, her body arching against him; all she knew was that she wanted more of him, needed more, ached for more.

Every fibre of her being throbbed, every nerve-end was full of sensation—and he had not yet begun!

Suddenly everything changed. A mutual animal hunger carried them along on a wave of frenzied desire, teeth and tongues meeting and exploring and tasting, his mouth ravaging hers, his body setting her on fire.

'God,' he breathed into her mouth, 'how I've dreamt of this moment. How much I've wanted you.'

And the truth of the matter was that she also wanted

him. She had never felt more feminine, nor ached with such a desperate longing. She was twenty-three years old and had never known that such delights of the body existed!

His hand moved to the buttons on her dress, sliding them undone one by one, kissing each inch of flesh as it was exposed, looking at her occasionally to see if she was going to stop him. But Melissa was too far gone. A fire that he had lit raged inside her, and only he could assuage it.

When all the buttons were undone he slid her dress over her shoulders, tracing the shape of her breasts lightly with trembling fingertips, exploring, looking at her with wonder in his dark eyes. 'You're so beautiful, Melissa.'

In answer she gave another moan. He was quite something himself. And why was he waiting? Why was he so gentle? So slow?

His thumb and forefinger tightened about a hardened nipple, his eyes watching her face closely for her reaction, and she arched her throat and took in a much needed breath of air. God, it was mind-shattering!

But it was even more achingly devastating when he took her nipples one by one into his mouth, his tongue and teeth teasing, sending desire screaming round her body. Her loins ached so much, and she strained against him, feeling his arousal, too, knowing that she wanted him to carry their lovemaking to its ultimate conclusion.

'Oh, Benedict, I never knew it could be like this.' The words tumbled involuntarily from her, her hands holding his head, her eyes glazed from the sheer intensity of her arousal.

'I've not yet started,' he said throatily. 'This is just

a taste of what we can enjoy together.' He lifted his head, his mouth soft and moist from licking and kissing her breasts. 'I never thought this day would come. I thought you would fight me for ever.' His lips moved once again to claim hers, his hands on her back, crushing her against him. 'I can't put into words how much I want you. You're so lovely, so sexy, so——'

His words tailed off as the door pushed open. 'I thought I heard voices. I——' Vivienne clapped a hand to her mouth as she came into the room and saw them. 'Oh, I'm sorry, I didn't realise—— I'll go, don't let me interrupt.'

But she had interrupted already, and Melissa was glad. Vivienne's appearance had brought her to her senses. What had happened? She was insane letting Benedict do this to her. He wanted her, he said. *He wanted her!* And if Vivienne hadn't disturbed them he would have had her.

CHAPTER SIX

BENEDICT would have kissed her again if Melissa had not pulled away and started to tug her dress back up over her shoulders.

'Melissa? Melly?' His tone was soft and persuasive. 'What's wrong?'

'This is wrong, you and me,' she cried. 'I don't want you to kiss me, I don't want to get involved.'

'There are some things you cannot help,' he pointed out.

How true that was. And responding to Benedict was one of them. 'I'm not ready for anything like this yet,' she protested. 'Surely you can understand that?'

His breath whistled through his teeth, and his eyes grew suddenly cold. 'Don't keep feeding me that one.'

'You still think I'm having an affair with Clifford?' Melissa glared, wondering how such intense desire could fade so quickly.

'You don't leave me much choice.' His expression was one of disgust.

She finished fastening the buttons on her dress. 'If you want to go on thinking that way then that's your prerogative, but I can assure you there's nothing but friendship between Clifford and me.'

His chest rose as he drew in a deep breath. 'OK, Melissa, I believe you.' But he did not sound as though he

91

meant it.

He took her face between his palms and looked deep into her eyes, and then he kissed her. A light kiss, the sort Clifford gave her, nothing sexual. 'I think it's time I went.'

Melissa locked the door behind him and went up to her room, undressing slowly and getting into bed. Benedict had stirred alien feelings inside her. She could feel his hands and mouth still on her breasts. If she closed her eyes she could relive every delicious moment. Why, then, had she stopped him? Why had she not let him carry on?

She did not need to tell herself the answer. She knew. Sex was such a violent emotion that if she got involved with Benedict she might never be able to face the world without him again. She had already lost one man, though it was slowly dawning on her that the loss might not be as great as she had at first imagined. But she did not want to commit herself to Benedict only to find that he would discard her, too. Why, oh why, couldn't she love Clifford? Then everything would be all right.

The next morning Vivienne apologised for intruding on them. 'I had no idea things were like that between you, none at all.' The older woman looked very happy.

'They are not like that,' corrected Melissa. 'Letting Benedict kiss me was a mistake, and one I'm not likely to make again. In fact I'm glad you came in. You stopped me making a complete fool of myself.'

'I see,' said Vivienne, and some of the pleasure faded from her eyes. 'But you could do worse. Benedict's a——'

'Please, don't sing his praises any more,' interjected Melissa. 'I know you think the world of him, but he's not right for me.'

'And how do you know he's not?' frowned the older

woman.

'I just know,' insisted Melissa.

Wisely Vivienne changed the subject.

They had a full day ahead of them. Clifford was due at ten to discuss the storyboards for his new diamond commercial. Melissa was expected to be present, and as she had seen none of the artwork yet she felt very excited.

In the middle of the presentation Melissa noticed Benedict standing quietly at the back of the room. A warmth stole through her as fleeting memories of last night returned, but before she could even acknowledge his presence Clifford demanded her attention.

Melissa was impressed with the quality of the artwork. Vivienne's art director and his team had certainly captured the image she wanted to convey, even down to the as yet faceless body, which had the hard, tanned toughness of Benedict's own. It was incredible. Or was it simply her imagination?

Clifford suggested one or two minor alterations, and he never stopped congratulating her on her original idea, and when Melissa finally looked Benedict's way again he had gone. She could not describe the disappointment she felt.

Lunch was a sandwich and coffee affair while more details were discussed. Melissa discovered that Clifford the businessman was very different to the sensitive companion who had wined and dined her these past weeks. He knew what he wanted and went all out for it. There were no half measures.

Vivienne decided to work late that evening and Melissa went home alone. Benedict was sitting out in the garden enjoying the late afternoon sun. 'Why did you rush off?'

asked Melissa at once, a thrill coursing through her at the mere sight of him.

His brows rose and he eyed her coldly. 'I came to ask you out to lunch—until I saw you were otherwise engaged.' His tone was damning.

Melissa heaved an exasperated sigh. 'Don't say we're back on Clifford again. It was purely business today, Benedict, as you well know.'

'I saw the way he was looking at you.'

'And how was that ?' she demanded.

'God, if you couldn't see it,' he crashed out, 'then you must be blind.'

Melissa lifted her chin haughtily. 'I think you see what you want to see.'

'You're seeing too much of him,' snarled Benedict. 'I don't think he's good for you.'

'And you are, I suppose?' she countered fiercely.

'Last night I thought——'

'Last night you kissed me against my will. Something Clifford Drew would never do.'

His eyes darkened and she observed the way his fingers curled into his palms. It was a habit of his when he was angry. 'I didn't notice you stopping me,' he grated.

Melissa shrugged. 'I was grateful for Vivienne's interruption—and you know why. I was insane ever to let you touch me.'

'You enjoyed it. You even admitted that it had never been that good with Tim. So what are you trying to prove? That you've given up sex altogether?' His lips twisted in a sneer. 'If I wanted to, Melissa, I could have you melting in my arms right now.'

'Don't be so sure,' she retorted, even though deep down

inside she knew it was true.

'But it's no fun taking a woman who's not willing,' he flung dismissively, 'so you're quite safe.'

'Thanks for nothing.' She lifted her chin and walked haughtily back into the house. What an arrogant swine he was.

The phone rang; it was Vivienne. 'Melly, love, I won't be home for dinner.'

'Surely you're not going to work late?' frowned Melissa.

'No, I'm almost finished,' said Vivienne cheerfully. 'Meredith's just phoned and invited me over to his place. Expect me when you see me.' The line went dead.

Melissa had a sneaking suspicion that Vivienne had arranged this deliberately. She knew Melissa had no date with Clifford tonight. Maybe she was hoping Benedict would come down. She might even have suggested it to him.

Her premonition came true when a short while later the phone rang and Benedict invited her up to his flat for dinner.

'No, thanks,' she said promptly.

'Any particular reason why not?'

'I don't want to.'

'But I'd like you to. I happen to know that you're alone, and I've cooked enough for the two of us. I've already unlocked the adjoining door. I'll see you in ten minutes.' And the line went dead.

It was twenty minutes later before Melissa finally went up to Benedict's flat. She had fought a battle with herself and lost.

She climbed the stairs and he met her and led her into

his living-room. It was a huge room with a table at one
end already laid. There were even candles on it, black
ones, in white holders, and a bowl of white roses from
Vivienne's garden. It was starkly simple, yet beautiful.
The whole room was beautiful, antique and modern
furniture mingling harmoniously.

'I was about to come and fetch you,' he said his eyes
serious.

Melissa shrugged. 'I almost didn't come.'

'I would have dragged you here.'

And she could see that he meant it. He wore a pair of
casual summer slacks this evening, and a half-sleeve
cotton shirt with a blue stripe. They accentuated the
breadth and height of him, his strength, his sexuality.
There was absolutely no ignoring it.

Then he smiled suddenly and her heart contracted and
she wondered why she was fighting him.

'An aperitif?' he asked, but she shook her head. 'In that
case, please sit down.'

He had laid places opposite each other and throughout
the meal his eyes were rarely off her face. They began
with a clear vegetable soup, which he freely admitted had
come out of a tin, and this was followed by Dover sole
with new potatoes and peas and parsley sauce, which was
absolutely delicious.

'Tell me about yourself, Melissa,' he said. 'I know
about Tim, and that you have a sister, but I still don't
know very much about you as a person, your likes and
dislikes, your hobbies, your ambition.'

Melissa shrugged. 'There's not much to tell. There's
only one thing I really hate, and that's men who take me
for granted, men who force themselves on me, men who

build up my hopes and then let me down.'

'In fact all men?'

'Most men,' she corrected. 'There are exceptions.'

'Clifford Drew for one?'

'Clifford,' she admitted. 'And there must be others who I've not yet met.'

'And which list am I on?'

She held his gaze. 'You can work that out for yourself. What else did you ask me? Oh, yes, hobbies. I like painting and drawing, and I used to write poetry.'

'How very talented you are. Did you have anything to do with those storyboards that I saw this morning?'

'Heavens, no,' she cried. 'I'm not that good.'

'But the commercial was your idea?'

He sounded bitter and she wondered why. 'Yes.'

'Why didn't you tell me about it?'

Melissa arched her brows. 'If I remember rightly, I did suggest that you needed a more romantic theme, but you gave the impression you wouldn't be interested. Besides, I hadn't actually thought it up then.'

'And when did this—brilliant idea come to you?'

When I was crying on your chest! What would he say if she told him that? She smiled. 'Oh, I don't know. It just sort of popped into my mind.'

'It's different,' he admitted. 'Clifford likes it, does he?'

'He's over the moon. All we have to do now is find the right man for the part.'

She cut into her fish and lifted her fork to her mouth and found his eyes disturbingly on her.

'Did you have anyone in mind—when the thought came to you?'

A slow warmth stole beneath Melissa's skin and her

heart began an urgent tattoo. 'Not really.'

'That's odd. I would have thought you had a picture image of the man, that it was perhaps your own hand that was touching his body. Perhaps someone like Tim, or Clifford? Someone you know very well, intimately even. Perhaps you're even relating it to a situation that you've already been in?'

Melissa closed her eyes, hating him, but contrarily feeling excited by his taunting tone.

'I can see I'm not far off the mark. Tell me more, Melissa. Tell me who the lucky man is.'

'You'd never believe me in a thousand years,' she said with saccharine sweetness.

'You could try me.'

'No, thanks,' she returned politely. 'Let's change the subject. Do you realise I know nothing at all about you, either? I didn't even know Viv had a godson until I came here.'

'Otherwise you would have come long before now to take a look at me?'

'On the contrary, I would have steered clear for the rest of my life,' she returned smartly.

He clapped a hand dramatically to his heart. 'How the lady likes to hurt. OK, so what is it you want to know? Age? Thirty-five. Height? Six-two. Weight? Twelve stone two. Marital status? Single. Health? Excellent. Anything else?'

She could not help smiling. 'You know that's not what I mean. I want to know where you were brought up, whether you went to university, whether you have any brothers or sisters, whether your parents are still alive, that sort of thing.'

'My father died when I was nine,' he said softly. 'My mother remarried a long time ago. They live near Colchester. I have an older sister who is married and lives in America. I got my *BA* at Oxford. I play rugby when I get the chance. I like girls with chestnut hair and green eyes. I——'

'That will do,' laughed Melissa.

'You think I don't mean it?'

'I think you're just saying it to make me feel good.'

'And has it worked?'

A quiver rode through her as their eyes met and held for a moment. God, did she feel good. Sitting this close, talking without arguing, his masculinity assailing her senses like a drug. She felt like a new woman. She was more aware of him than ever before.

'I feel flattered,' she said.

'Is that all?' He looked disappointed.

She nodded. It was as much as she was prepared to admit. 'There is one other thing I'd like to know. Why have you never married?'

His lips twisted. 'Let's say I've never met anyone who I've felt sufficiently interested in to want a permanent relationship.'

Her brows rose. 'You must be mighty choosy?'

He shrugged. 'Maybe I am—or maybe it's that I've never come across the right person.'

Melissa sipped her wine and looked at him over the rim of her glass. 'What sort of qualities would she need, this perfect woman?'

'Oh, I don't know,' he said, sitting back in his chair and searching the ceiling for an answer. 'She would need to be understanding—I'm away from home a lot.

Certainly never jealous—I meet a lot of pretty girls. Looks don't enter into it so long as she has the right sort of personality. A good conversationalist, intelligent, thoughtful, a good homemaker and mother—I'd like lots of children.' His lips quirked.

'She sounds as though she would need to be a saint,' said Melissa.

'Oh, I don't think so,' he replied. 'How about you, Melissa. Do you want a family?'

'Yes, of course,' she answered at once. 'Two at the very least, probably three.'

'Then you do intend getting married?' There was a gleam in his eye as he spoke. 'You don't intend shutting men out of your life for ever?'

With an inward groan Melissa realised how neatly he had trapped her. 'That would be stupid, wouldn't it, saying a thing like that? I shall get over Tim—eventually. And I do realise that all men aren't the same, even though my own family seem to have the knack of picking the wrong ones.'

'I think you're already over Tim,' he said.

'Why, because I'm going out with Clifford?'

He frowned and Melissa wished she had not mentioned the other man's name. 'Partly, but that wasn't what I had in mind.'

It was Melissa's turn to frown. 'What were you thinking then?'

'About the way you returned my kisses last night. You would never have responded like that if you'd still been hungering after Tim. It's my guess you've already realised he was no big deal.'

'Maybe so,' admitted Melissa, 'but that doesn't mean

I'm ready to have an affair with you.'

'Who's talking about affairs?'

'What are you talking about, then?' she demanded, colour surging into her cheeks. He must think she had sex on the brain.

'I'm talking about trust. You obviously trust Clifford, though for the life of me I can't see why. Don't you think it's about time you learned to trust me?'

'It's not that easy,' she said huskily.

'Why?'

'Because you're trying to force me into a relationship I'm not ready for.

'Oh, Melissa,' he groaned. 'I think you're very ready. It's just a matter of learning to let go, to relax, to forget all the harsh thoughts you have about me.'

'You do turn me on,' she admitted, 'more than Tim ever did, in fact, but I need more out of a relationship than that.'

'What do you need?' His gaze never left her face.

'Understanding, patience, kindness.' And patience was definitely not one of Benedict's virtues.

'And I suppose Clifford has all those qualities?' he rasped, his eyes narrowed now. 'Does he turn you on as well? Is he the ultimate? Is he the man you've been looking for?'

Melissa pushed herself to her feet. 'I think it's time I went.'

'I take it my questions were too near the mark?' he snarled, and then, with a sudden change of tone, 'Don't go yet, Melissa. The night's young.'

She hesitated. 'I'll only stay if you promise not to mention Clifford.'

'I have a raspberry pavlova for pudding. Defrosted by my own fair hands. Do you want some?'

She could not help smiling. 'Yes, please.'

And the mood was set for the rest of the evening. She helped him wash up and afterwards he played records and they talked, while they drank coffee and more coffee. It was with reluctance that Melissa eventually said she must go.

Why couldn't he always be like that? He had been a perfect companion. He hadn't once pushed himself on her, although an air of sexual excitement had been present that was missing from her relationship with Clifford.

He walked back down with her to the communicating door, kissed her gravely and gently, then deliberately locked the door.

She went straight to her bedroom, her whole body a mass of sensation. What he had been doing to her tonight amounted to sheer torture. He had made it obvious by every word and every glance that he desired her, he had made her aware of him in every way possible, all without so much as laying one finger on her.

She would never have believed it possible. She wanted him as much now, if not more, as when he had kissed her. Her loins ached, her breasts ached, every inch of her was attuned to him. For goodness' sake, what sort of man was he who could do this to her?

In the days that followed Melissa made sure she kept out of his way by going out with Clifford every evening, much to the other man's delight and Benedict's disapproval.

'What the hell are you playing at?' he demanded,

coming storming into her office almost a week later. 'Why this infatuation with Clifford? What's the big attraction?'

He looked so angry that Melissa felt a shiver of fear. 'I don't see what it has to do with you.'

'No, I didn't think you would,' he snarled, 'but I have no intention of sitting back and letting you make a fool of yourself any longer. If you don't stop seeing him I shall have a word with Clifford myself. This is a ridiculous state of affairs. It's total insanity. The man's using you.'

Melissa felt a strange thrill of excitement. There was something about Benedict in this mood that aroused all her base emotions. She would love him to kiss her now, to feel the strength of his anger, the mighty power that radiated through him.

Her eyes sparked green fire, her lips parted. 'You sound jealous.'

'Maybe I am,' he rasped fiercely. 'You shun me like a dog with rabies, and yet you let that lecherous beast put his hands all over you.'

'Now wait a minute.' Melissa began to grow angry herself. 'Clifford's not like that.'

'So you keep telling me. But I shall never believe you, not in a thousand years. Take a good look at yourself, Melissa. How could any man keep his hands off you?'

'And not in a thousand years will I take any notice of what you say,' she threw at him furiously, thankful Vivienne had already gone home. Another few seconds and she would have gone herself. What fate had made her stay on to file those letters? The whole building was most probably empty now. There were just the two of them.

'It's none of your damned business what I do with my

life,' she continued. 'Just get out of it, will you. Stop watching over me like a father figure.'

'Hell, Melly, I have no paternal feelings for you, and you know it.' He closed the space between them and pulled her hard against him. His mouth swooped on hers and every ounce of passion and anger that was in him was put into that kiss.

Melissa's anger melted instantly and, after a first instinct to fight free, she gave herself up to the aching pleasure of his kiss. Brutal and punishing though it was, it clawed its way along her nerve-streams until her whole body pulsed with desire.

'Is this how Clifford does it?' he breathed against her mouth. 'Does he kiss you like this? And touch you like this?' His hand closed on her breast, but the hindrance of her blouse angered him and buttons popped as he sought her naked skin.

Melissa could do nothing to stop him. He was neither punishing nor hurting her, even though it was probably what he intended. Instead he was exciting and inflaming her. They were like two hungry animals, greedily taking whatever the other offered, and what wasn't offered as well!

With a strangled cry Benedict lifted her into his arms and carried her through into Vivienne's office and towards the wide couch. 'I've waited long enough,' he groaned, his lips continuing their assault.

But aroused as she was Melissa had no intention of letting him go any further. 'Stop it, Benedict, *stop it!* Put me down. At once.'

'Why should I?' he jeered. 'Why the hell should I? You haven't fought me one little bit. You've proved what sort of a girl you are. Don't go prudish on me now, because it won't work.'

It was true, she had wanted him. She had enjoyed every heart-thudding second, but not this—she did not want him to take her in anger.

'You're going to rape me then, are you?' she thrust derisively. 'Because that's what it will amount to, Benedict, and what will your devoted godmother say then? You can't do a thing wrong in her eyes, you should know that. But rape? Well, I guess that would pretty well disgust her. And yourself, too, once you came to your senses. But if it will really do you good——' with a tremendous effort she made herself go limp in his arms '—then take me.'

With a strangled oath he dropped her, stumbling noisily out of the office and slamming the door behind him.

Melissa sat down, every pulse throbbing, every limb trembling. It was her own fault. She should have known better than to taunt Benedict.

Eventually she crawled back into her own office, gathered up her jacket and bag, and went home. Vivienne took one look at her pale face and put on the kettle, spooning coffee into a mug and saying nothing until Melissa had drunk it all up.

'Now suppose you tell me what's wrong?'

'It's nothing. Just Benedict, making a nuisance of himself,' said Melissa, shrugging her shoulders and trying to pass it off. 'If you'll excuse me I must go and get ready.'

'You're seeing Clifford again tonight?'

She nodded.

Vivienne shook her head. 'Do you really think it's wise, seeing so much of him?'

And because Melissa was still raw, because Benedict had aroused her against her will and she hated him for it, she turned sharply on the older woman.

'That's rich, coming from you. Don't forget you were the one to introduce us. You were the one who said I should go out with him in the first place.' Her eyes blazed and she could not stop herself trembling.

Vivienne looked shocked by the ferocity of Melissa's outburst. 'Yes, but——'

'But nothing,' cried Melissa. 'I like Clifford very much. We have a lot in common. We get on well together. He'll never hurt me, nor let me down. He's my friend and I need him and if I want to see him every night then that's my business. Just leave me alone, will you?' And with that she burst into tears.

Instantly the other woman's arms went about her. 'Melly, love, what's wrong? Why are you so worked up? I merely wanted to point out that it's not wise to devote all your time to one man.'

'But I feel safe with Clifford,' protested Melissa.

Vivienne nodded. 'I realise that, love, but I think the time has come to go out with other men now. Clifford helped you when you needed someone, but you can't hang on to him for ever.'

Melissa scowled. 'I don't want to go out with Benedict, if that's what you're thinking. He's just told me off about Clifford as well. I hate him.'

Vivienne closed her eyes and let out an angry breath. 'No wonder you're so uptight. I imagine he didn't mince words. He's like a cat on hot bricks every time you're out with Clifford, do you know that? He comes down here and wants to know where you are and what time you went and when I'm expecting you back.'

'I hope you tell him to mind his own business,' snapped Melissa.'

'Just think about what I've said,' advised Vivienne softly.

Melissa knew they were both right, that she was not being fair either on Clifford or herself by seeing so much of him. He was beginning to depend on her; he was beginning to read too much into their relationship. And one day he would get hurt. She didn't want to do that to him. He had been hurt once, when his wife died; it was unfair to build up his hopes. But she could not stop seeing him. She needed him.

The next day Benedict and Vivienne were in consultation in Vivienne's office all morning. At lunchtime she sent out for sandwiches and invited Melissa to join them.

'I have some good news,' she smiled. 'We begin shooting the commercials for Drew's diamonds next week.'

'You do?' Melissa's eyes widened. She knew things were moving quickly, but had no idea they were at this stage. 'How wonderful. Where? Can I watch?' She had never seen an actual commercial in the making.

'But of course you're going to be there. This is your baby, Melly.'

Melissa glanced across at Benedict and saw the speculative gleam in his eyes. Something churned inside her.

'Aren't you curious as to who has been chosen to play

the lucky man?' His tone held a hint of mockery, missed by Vivienne but very, very clear to Melissa.

She shrugged, attempting indifference. 'I don't think who it is matters, so long as he has the right physical attributes.'

Her eyes were caught and held by his and she felt herself grow hot. Lord, don't say he had volunteered himself—and she had to watch some other girl touching him, feeling him, playing up to him?'

In that instant Melissa realised how much she wanted Benedict. Her whole body craved him. Even now, in front of Vivienne, she was responding to his overpowering sexuality. But she still refused to accept that it was love she felt for him. It was nothing more than an intense, painful, physical attraction. One she must fight at all costs.

'That's right,' said Vivienne, unaware that she was cutting through tension. 'That's why we're choosing as yet unknown male models.'

Relief flooded over Melissa and Benedict saw it and smiled secretly. Damn him! she thought. He had known exactly what she was thinking.

'More than one?' she frowned.

'That's right,' confirmed Vivienne. 'We're using a different man for each separate commercial in the campaign. And each ad is going to be shot in a different location.' She paused and smiled. 'Aren't you going to ask me where?'

Melissa nodded. 'I can't wait to hear.'

'Paris, Amsterdam, Rome, Venice. All the world's most romantic cities. Clifford really wants us to go to town.'

Benedict was forgotten. Melissa sat forward on the edge of her seat. 'And I'm going to see them being made? I'm going to all those wonderful places?'

Vivienne smiled at the younger girl's enthusiasm. 'Every one of them. Starting with Paris next week.'

Melissa could not believe her good fortune. 'Is Clifford going, too?' He had said nothing to her last night.

Out of the corner of her eye she saw Benedict's face harden, and even Vivienne frowned slightly. 'No, Clifford won't be coming. Just you and me.'

Later Melissa wondered whether this wasn't Vivienne's method of getting her away from Clifford. She had never expected to be involved in the filming of the commercial. It was a complete surprise, but an exciting one, and she was really looking forward to it.

That night when she saw Clifford she was bubbling with excitement. 'Guess what, I'm going to Paris next week to see the first of your commercials being filmed.'

He took one look at her glowing face and said, 'I'm very pleased for you, Melly. But I shall miss you, you do know that?'

She nodded ruefully. 'I'm not really being fair on you, am I? I've seen such a lot of you lately and yet I don't think I shall ever love you, Clifford, not how you love me. I'm so sorry.'

He put a finger to her lips. 'Don't say that. I've told you, it doesn't matter. There's a vast difference in you now from when we first met. If I'm helping you regain your trust, that's what's important—for now, anyway. But I shall never give up hope. So long as there's no one else?'

'No.' She shook her head vigorously, too vigorously perhaps, for he frowned faintly. But there wasn't anyone, was there? What she felt for Benedict was a purely sexual thing, nothing to do with love.

Then he smiled. 'You enjoy yourself and I'll be waiting when you come back. Think of me a little. Perhaps you'll even find time to phone me?' He kissed her gently on the mouth, but he was trembling and Melissa knew how much she meant to him. How unfair life was. Why couldn't she love this kind, gentle man?

The days sped by and soon there was only one more to go before they left. Melissa was careful to keep out of Benedict's way; she knew what would happen if they got together. Their hunger for each other was like a time bomb waiting to go off. She had never experienced anything like it before. But damn him, she was not going to give herself to a man who did not love her, no matter how great their feelings were.

There was so much work to be cleared up before they left that Melissa felt exhausted. It did not matter to Vivienne that Benedict was there to look after things; she wanted to sort everything out herself. She liked her finger on every pulse. Melissa did not know where she found her energy.

Then all of a sudden, rushing out of her office to hand Melissa some last-minute typing, Vivienne's heel somehow caught in the edge of the metal strip that fixed the carpet across the doorway, and with a cry she plunged heavily to the floor.

Melissa was at her side in an instant. 'My ankle,' Vivianne cried. 'Oh, God, it hurts. I think I must have broken it.'

Every vestige of colour drained from Vivienne's face and she was evidently in a lot of pain. Melissa helped her to sit up against the door-jamb. 'Don't move, I'll phone for an ambulance.'

Vivienne's hands were on her outstretched leg, her eyes closed, beads of perspiration on her upper lip. She waited until Melissa had come off the phone, then she said faintly, 'Paris, Melissa. Paris! What am I going to do about the Paris trip? I must be there. No one else is capable of handling it.' She attempted to struggle to her feet.

'Never mind Paris,' exclaimed Melissa impatiently, holding her firmly down. 'It can wait. Lord, your health's more important than some silly stupid advertisement.'

'Silly? Stupid?' Vivienne attempted to smile. 'It was your idea.'

'And my idea now is that we get you to hospital. For goodness' sake sit still.' Vivienne's ankle was already swelling at an alarming rate. She could imagine how painful it must be—and yet still all the woman could think about was work.

The ambulance arrived and Vivienne was taken to hospital, Melissa following in her car. The ankle was X-rayed and it was diagnosed not as a fracture but a sprain. Their relief was short-lived, however, when the doctor said she would need to keep off it for several weeks.

'There's only one thing for it,' said Vivienne after hearing the news. 'Filming Clifford's commercial can't possibly wait that long. Benedict will have to go in my place.'

'I'll stay with you, of course,' said Melissa at once.

But Vivienne would not hear of it.

CHAPTER SEVEN

'PERFECT, beautiful, superb, exquisite!' The film director beamed all over his face and Melissa felt a moment's personal triumph.

What an experience it had been, watching these men work. Bert Maddox knew exactly how to coax the best out of everyone, yet even so it had taken him days to get it exactly right. The models' moods, the weather, the light, the exact camera angles. And now he was satisfied.

The filming had taken place in the Champ de Mars gardens beneath the Eiffel Tower, with the fountains playing, and all of Paris watching. Melissa had experienced quite a thrill as she saw the whole thing coming together. And when the beautiful girl's hand slid seductively over the male model's body she had relived memories of that time she had been held against Benedict. The moment her idea was born. Her tears on his chest had started it all off. If only he knew.

She gave a nervous jump when Benedict's voice came over her shoulder. 'I've been watching you, Melissa.' His tone was low and sensual. 'You lived every moment of that shot, didn't you? You experienced sensations that I'm quite sure the models themselves never felt.' His hands touched her shoulders. 'To them it was a job; to you—it was something more.' He spun her round, his dark smoky eyes studying her face.

Meliss felt a thrill ride through her. He had been subtly

seducing her ever since they arrived. She had done her best to fend him off, but it was difficult when they were thrust more and more together. Thank goodness this was it. The filming was finished. Now they could pack up and go home.

'Of course it was,' she said, meeting his gaze, doing her best to pretend nothing was happening to her. 'It was quite something seeing my thoughts come to life. Like a dream that turns to reality. I was totally fascinated.'

'So I noticed. What did you think of our male model? Did he turn you on? Is that what the light in your eyes is all about?' His eyes narrowed, his tone dropped to a low husky growl.

'Guy? Heavens, no!' It had not been Guy lying there, but Benedict. And it had not been Karen touching him, but herself. What would he make of that if she told him? 'It's excitement,' she retorted firmly. 'This is a totally new experience. I'm almost sorry we have to go home.'

'We don't have to,' he said.

Melissa's head jerked up. 'What do you mean?'

'We could stay on a few more days, just you and me.'

Her heart began to pound at the mere thought of it. Here in Paris she had seen a totally different side to Benedict. Although the whole film crew had stayed in the same hotel, and they had spent all of their time with them—Melissa had seen to that—Benedict had still managed to affect her like no other man ever had.

He had not overstepped the mark once, even though Melissa was perfectly sure it killed him being so good. His eyes, though, had told her how he felt, and the little thoughtful acts like arranging for early morning tea in her room, an English newspaper, the best table in the restaurant, her favourite wine, had not gone unnoticed.

'I imagine Vivienne wouldn't be too pleased,' she said.

'I spoke to Viv on the phone this morning. She's having a high old time, lording it from her sitting-room at home. She has an army of staff running to and fro from the house to her office. She has two telephone lines and a computer terminal. No way is that lady going to let go. She won't miss us, Melly.' The diminutive was an endearment, a caress; a subtle change in their relationship.

Her heart beat faster still, her pulses, too. It was tempting. There was a persistence about Benedict that she could not help admiring. Why not enjoy a few days? Hadn't her body been craving his ever since they met?

This was such an about-turn to her previous thoughts that it took even her by surprise, and her eyes widened as she looked at him.

He smiled briefly. 'Your answer is yes?'

Melissa closed her eyes, took a deep breath, and nodded. God help her. She hoped she would never regret it.

The next second she was crushed against his chest. For a brief moment only. Then he let her go and grinned and took her hand. 'Let's get back to the hotel. We'll shower and change and then we'll go out on the town.'

He sounded very triumphant. Was that how he saw it? A victory? An achievement? Perhaps it was. After all, she had been pretty hard on him.

In the days that followed Melissa enjoyed it all. A breath-taking ride up the Eiffel Tower, a stroll along the Champs-Elysées, a fascinating tour of Notre Dame, the Louvre and its museum. A never-to-be-forgotten evening at the Moulin Rouge. Scrambling on and off the Métro, laughing, holding hands, kissing, watching the inevitable couple of lovers who were totally oblivious to those around them.

It was a whole new world, and Melissa found a new happiness. Tim faded further and further into the background and she found herself wondering whether she hadn't some future with Benedict after all. He was not rushing her into anything she was not ready for, and she liked him all the more for it. Perhaps she had misjudged him.

Each night he came back to her room for a nightcap and they would talk about what they had done that day. His kisses grew from a chaste goodnight peck to more passionate embraces.

He loved it when the day ended and she took the pins out of her hair and it flowed freely and heavily about her face and shoulders. He buried his face in it, threaded his fingers through it, and used it to hold her his prisoner.

'You're very beautiful, Melly, do you know that?' His eyes were inches from her own and she melted into him. 'God, what you do to me!' His mouth claimed hers for the hundredth time that night.

And what he did to her, thought Melissa.

But always he held himself in check. Always their lovemaking never went any further than kissing and touching. She was aware of the strain on him and wondered from where he drew the strength. She wanted more. Perhaps she ought to instigate the lovemaking herself? But always she fought shy. She was not sure she would know how to handle such a situation.

One day, when they got back to the hotel to shower and

change before going out for what Benedict had promised would be a memorable meal at one of Paris's most exclusive restaurants, a beautiful bouquet of pink and white roses arrived for her.

'*I am missing you. Love, Clifford,*' the card said. Melissa buried her face in the sweet fragrance. Wasn't he a darling? It made her realise how long she had been away. Over a week now. How time had flown. She filled a vase with water and stood the flowers in it, and then hurried to take her shower before Benedict came knocking on the door.

Mm, how good it felt, washing away the dust and grime of a day spent traipsing the streets of Paris. She was beginning to know every square inch of the city, and seen through the eyes of Benedict, it was something else. He was familiar with Paris, he had lived here for a time, and he was a veritable mine of information.

She was glad she had stayed on, though she did sometimes feel guilty about leaving Vivienne to cope alone. But whenever she phoned Viv always said that she was not to worry. Everything was under control and Melissa was just to concentrate on having a wonderful time.

Vivienne would say that, smiled Melissa to herself. Aunt Viv had such high hopes for her and Benedict. Her mind must be running riot.

Melissa was humming happily to herself as she left the bathroom and moved through into the lounge, her body roughly towelled dry. She intended taking another sniff at those gorgeous roses before she got dressed.

Then suddenly the door was pushed open and Benedict walked in. Evidently the porter had not closed it properly and Benedict must have assumed she had left it open for him.

She froze in her tracks and he looked at her, at every inch of her naked body, right from the tip of her painted toenails, up her long legs, over her flat stomach and her heavy breasts, lingering a moment on her taut nipples, right up to her hair which she had piled on top of her head while taking her shower.

And the odd part about it was that she did not feel shy or embarrassed. She grew warm all over, her heart thudded and her whole body responded.

'God, Melly.' That was all he said before he was across the room and had pulled her into his arms. His breathing was ragged, his kisses urgent, and the control he had exercised these last days had at last broken.

There was a fierce hunger now in his kisses, his mouth and tongue ravaging hers, his hands touching and exploring, and she felt as though she was melting. All sane reasoning fled as she parted her lips, moaning her pleasure at his hungry exploration. He had waited so long for this moment that there was no tenderness in him now, and she wanted none. She was as desperate as he was.

For an instant he held her from him, his smouldering eyes again raking every curve and contour. 'Melly, you're beautiful. And how I want you!'

Fresh floods of sensation massed inside her. She pressed herself into him, her loins on fire. This was the moment. This was the moment she had been waiting for ever since he had suggested they spend a few days alone.

Their hunger was mutual. She shuddered with pure passion, her head flung back, her throat arched as he bit and teased. She cried out with the sheer exquisite pleasure of feelings so intense she felt she was going to die, feelings she had never, ever, experienced in her whole life before.

She arched her body closer and closer, murmuring his name over and over again, holding his head, feeling the thickness of his hair, and wanting him, oh, so desperately.

When his hand moved down over her stomach and hips, to her inner thighs, to the intimate places no man had ever been, a moan was wrenched from her. Oh, God, how could she stand such exquisite pleasure, or was it torture? She arched herself into him as ripple after ripple of sheer animal hunger washed over her.

And then suddenly, from nowhere, came the thought that this was too big a step to take. She couldn't go through with it. She would be committing herself—and she was still not ready for anything like that.

She stiffened in his arms and at first Benedict seemed not to notice. Then he paused and frowned and looked into her face. 'Melly? Am I hurting you?'

She shook her head.

'What then? Lord, don't say no now. Melly, I've been patient so long. You've no idea how much I've wanted you. All I've been waiting for is a signal that——' Then his eyes alighted on the flowers, and the card still lying on the table. He peered closer and let out a roar of anger, thrusting her from him.

'The bastard! He's the reason, isn't he? He's the reason you've held me off all this time. To think I genuinely believed there was nothing between you.'

'Benedict, there isn't.' Melissa cowered against the chair where she had stumbled, her eyes wide pools of green terror. She had never seen him this angry.

'No? You expect me to believe that?' He picked up the card and read it aloud. 'I am missing you. Love, Clifford.' He managed to make it sound dirty. 'Missing you! Missing what? Your lovemaking, your beautiful body in his arms? And he sends his love. How pathetic. But if he can have you then I'm darn sure I can.'

He lunged towards her, his eyes wild, his face an ugly red. Melissa tried to struggle to her feet but he was quicker than she and the next moment she was pinned to the floor beneath him.

'Benedict, no, please no.'

Her plea was in vain. She doubted he even heard her.

His hot mouth covered hers, his tongue urgent and demanding, his hands holding her face so that she could not move.

Then, still straddling her, he began struggling out of his clothes and Melissa's fear heightened. 'Benedict. *Benedict!* Please, stop! There's never been anything between me and Clifford. You must believe that. Please. We're friends, that's all. And of course he's missed me. We saw so much of each other.'

Finally her cries seemed to get through to him. He pushed himself to his feet, towering over her like an angry giant, his eyes smouldering with fire, his nostrils dilated, his mouth a thin grim line, his arms swinging loosely from his shoulders, fingers curled into fists. He breathed heavily and unevenly and was fighting a monumental inner battle.

Then with a despairing groan he lurched for the door, leaving it wide open as he disappeared into his own room next to hers.

Melissa shuddered and lay there for a moment until she realised what it would look like if anyone walked past. It was an effort to crawl across the room, and once the door was closed she leaned against it, wishing herself a thousand miles away.

She began to shiver and she went through to her bedroom and pulled on a robe, then she sat down on the bed. Gradually, as she grew calmer, she could see why Benedict had reacted as he had, how it must look to him, why he was so disgusted.

She would wait until he, too, had simmered down, then she would go to him, she would make him see sense, she would make him understand. Things had been going so well between them.

But it wasn't because of Clifford that she found it impossible to let him make love to her. It was her own deep-seated distrust that was destroying her. And until she overcame that she would never be able to give herself to any man.

She had thought she was over it. These last few days she had felt so at peace with Benedict. No, that was wrong. Not at peace. She had felt—at one with him. She had laughed and played and wanted to spend every second at his side. And yet look what had happened when his lovemaking became too possessive. What was wrong with her? Please couldn't someone tell her?

Melissa gradually grew calm enough to get dressed but it was another hour before she dared venture to contact Benedict. She tapped on his door, then knocked more loudly. 'Benedict. Benedict! I want to talk to you.'

But although she heard him moving about inside and he snarled something that sounded suspiciously like an oath he did not open the door. 'Please, Benedict.' Melissa felt hurt by his behaviour. 'This is stupid. You can't go on ignoring me. It wasn't my fault.'

Again no response and Melissa felt like breaking the door down. He was being unreasonable. Clifford's gesture had been entirely innocent. Why couldn't he believe that? OK, Clifford did love her, but he knew there was no hope. He wasn't pestering her or anything like that, he was just letting her know that he still thought of her and was still there if she needed him.

She returned slowly to her room, her shoulders sagging. Clifford had asked her to phone him and she hadn't. Why not now? He was the one person she could rely on to restore her sanity.

He answered immediately and his deep gruff tone was at once familiar and reassuring.

'Clifford, it's me, Melissa.'

'Melly, my princess. How are you?'

'I got your flowers. They're lovely. Thank you, thank you so much.'

'Beautiful flowers for a beautiful lady. How're things going?'

Her pause was just a fraction too long. 'Oh, fine. Benedict knows Paris like the back of his hand.'

'Melly, is something wrong?'

Melissa closed her eyes. 'Not really. I just wanted to talk to you.'

'Are you trying to tell me something?' he asked, his tone suddenly quiet and hurt. 'About you and Benedict. Are you——'

'No,' she cut in at once, realising he thought she was going to say she had fallen in love with Benedict, that the magic of Paris had worked its spell on her. 'Nothing like that.'

He was silent a moment, as though not sure whether to believe her, then he said, 'Melly, I have to be honest. I was as jealous as hell when I found out you'd gone with Benedict instead of Vivienne, even though I knew it was purely business.'

'It was,' she stated firmly. 'I didn't want to go with him. It was the last thing I wanted.'

'And yet you stayed on, just the two of you. I've been beside myself, Melly. My mind's been running riot. I only want your happiness, you know that, but—Benedict?'

'Cliff, I'm not involved with Benedict, I'm not having an affair, or anything like that.' She tried to make her voice sound bright and convincing. 'We've had a wonderful few days.'

But she had not reckoned on Clifford's astuteness. 'Something's happened, though, hasn't it? All of a sudden you can't handle the situation.'

'Of course I can,' she said, though she knew she sounded less than convincing.

'Then why are you calling at this time of day? Shouldn't you be out to dinner with Benedict?'

'Actually we did have a few words,' she admitted.

'And now you're alone and dejected and, hell, Melly, my princess, you need me. You think I don't know you that well? I'm flying over. I'll be there just as soon as I can. Don't you fret any more. I'm on my way.'

'Cliff, no, I don't want you to do that, honestly, I just——' But she was talking to thin air. The line had gone dead.

She replaced the receiver, smiling ruefully. She had not intended that he should come here, she had just wanted to talk to him, to hear his soothing voice. But she should have known. He knew her too well to be deceived.

What would Benedict say when Clifford arrived? He would be angrier still, that was for sure. Not that she could do anything about it. If he didn't believe that her relationship with Clifford was entirely innocent, if he thought her a liar, then he was not the man for her. A good relationship had to be based on trust.

At this point in her thoughts Melissa grimaced. Who was she to talk? She had no right to condemn; she didn't trust Benedict. She trusted no man—except Clifford of course. He was different. He was her friend and comforter, and all of a sudden she was glad he was coming.

Not expecting him until some time the following morning, Melissa was absolutely astonished when reception rang through in the early hours to say that he had arrived. She wondered how he had managed it so quickly. Fortunately she had not gone to bed. There had seemed no point. She had known she would not sleep.

She opened the door in readiness and stood in the middle of the room waiting. He appeared in less than two minutes, lines of exhaustion on his face, but nevertheless looking familiar and reassuring.

'Melly.' He walked towards her with his arms outstretched.

'Oh, Cliff, how glad I am to see you.' And she meant it. It felt good to be held by him, to know that she could relax and be herself, that she need not worry that things might get out of hand. He would look after her, he would never let her get hurt.

A sudden sound made them both look towards the door. Melissa's heart plummeted when she saw Benedict. His face was a picture of anger and disgust and disbelief, and she knew that they had just confirmed what up till now could only have been supposition on his part.

And in that instant Melissa knew without a doubt that she was in love with him. Despite everything, his accusations and suspicions, her vow never to let herself get close to another man, despite all this, she had fallen deeply and irrevocably in love.

CHAPTER EIGHT

THE discovery that she had fallen in love with Benedict stunned Melissa. She had been aware of the danger right from the beginning and had fought hard against it. So why had it happened? And was it really possible to love a man and yet be afraid to let him make love to her?

She knew why she was afraid—she still did not and could not trust him. Admittedly during those few days in Paris he had shown her a different side to his nature. She had seen a caring and thoughtful man, nothing had been too much trouble. He had wanted her to have a good time, and she had. And in doing so she had fallen in love.

At that moment there was nothing attractive about him. His face was ugly with anger, his eyes full of hostility and condemnation, his whole body tense with rage. She wondered why her relationship with Clifford mattered to him. Surely Benedict's feelings went no deeper than sexual desire, so why the unreasonable displays of temperament?

'What's wrong, Clifford, don't you trust her with me?' he thrust savagely, his voice thick with disgust. 'Couldn't you wait to get your filthy hands on her again?'

Melissa struggled out of Clifford's embrace and before he had the chance to defend himself, she rounded on Benedict, her eyes indignant, her whole body bristling. 'What a despicable mind you have, Benedict Burton.'

'I know what I saw,' he said, 'and I know what Clifford's message said.' He picked up the gold-fluted card and thrust it under Clifford's nose.

'Melly is a very dear and close friend,' Clifford said, 'but I haven't been to bed with her, if that's what you're thinking. I respect her too much.'

Benedict's eyes reflected his scepticism. 'You expect me to believe that? What man would fly nearly three hundred miles in the middle of the night to see a—friend? Especially when she's with another man. I'll tell you why. Because you're jealous. You regard her as your own private property. Isn't that right?'

His face was growing harder by the minute, his attitude more menacing. The hairs on the back of Melissa's neck began to stand up; she went deathly cold. What was happening to him?

But Clifford was more amused than anything else. 'I'm sure Melissa is pleased to see me.'

Benedict frowned and then turned on her accusingly. 'Are you, Melissa? *Are you?*'

'I'm always pleased to see Clifford,' she said honestly, silently praying that Benedict wouldn't let his temper run away with him.

'And was his coming here at this ungodly hour a complete surprise?' His eyes darted from one to the other, watching closely their reaction.

Melissa could not hide the truth. 'Not exactly.'

'He phoned and told you he was coming?'

She remained silent.

'You asked him to come?' There was incredulity in his voice.

'Not exactly, but I did phone him,' admitted Melissa

quietly.

He let out an angry breath and crashed a fist into his palm. 'Why? Dammit, why? No, don't tell me, I can guess. It's as I thought, isn't it? You prefer him to me.'

There was a fierce light in his eyes and Melissa sought Clifford's hand, her face paling. 'That's not true. You heard what Clifford said. We're good friends.'

Benedict eyed the clasped fingers. 'It looks like it.'

'That will do,' snapped Clifford suddenly and coldly. 'I think you've upset Melissa enough.'

Benedict eyed the other man venomously and for just a second she thought he was going to strike Clifford. Then to her surprise he abruptly turned and disappeared. She felt only faint releif. He would be back. They had not heard the last, she was sure.

Unable to help herself she burst into tears. Clifford put his arms about her, murmuring words of comfort. 'You love Benedict, don't you?' His tone was resigned.

Melissa nodded sadly, wondering how he had known when she had only just found out herself.

'I'm sorry it's not me,' he said gruffly. 'I think I knew all along that it was Benedict you wanted. You spoke about him so often.'

'Did I?' She frowned.

He nodded.

Melissa dabbed at her eyes with his handkerchief. 'I didn't know. But it's no good, he doesn't love me. He just wants to get me into bed.'

'Is that what all this was about.'

She grimaced. 'I'm afraid so. I wouldn't let him make love to me, then he spotted your flowers and immediately assumed it was because I preferred you to him.'

'A natural conclusion,' he said. 'I'd have done the same thing myself. I'm sorry I came now. I've made things worse, haven't I?'

'Not at all,' she said quickly, 'but I'm beginning to realise what I've put you through. I've been very selfish. I used you, knowing all along that you loved me and I could never return it. I'm truly sorry.'

'Don't be,' he said. 'You were open with me from the start. It was a chance I took. OK, I lost. But I'm still your friend, and I still want your happiness more than anything else. Actually I think Benedict does love you, even though he won't admit it, even to himself.'

'No!' She shook her head, refusing to believe him.

'Yes, Melly. He's one hell of a jealous guy, believe me.'

Melissa was silent a moment, then she squared her shoulders and stood tall and determined. 'Are you staying here tonight? Have you booked in?'

He nodded.

'Good. I think I might still need you.'

He took her face between his hands and kissed her forehead. She saw pain in his eyes but all he said was, 'I'll be here.'

And then he left her and she went to bed and to her amazement fell immediately asleep.

She slept late the next morning and was awoken by someone knocking on the door. She pulled on her robe and there was Clifford, freshly shaven, smiling, surprised to see her still in her nightclothes. 'I'm too early?'

'Not at all,' she said. 'Come in. It won't take me long to get ready.' He wore an open-necked shirt and smelled faintly of soap, and Melissa wished he were Benedict.

She closed her bedroom door and took a shower, and was in the middle of getting dressed when there was a knock at the door again. She called out to Clifford, 'Will you answer it, please? It's probably the maid come to clean. I'm usually out by now.'

Then she heard Benedict's voice and loud words between them before her door was rudely pushed open. Benedict's face was as black as a thundercloud. 'As I thought,' he rasped. 'Had a good night, did you?'

The disgust in his tone made her flinch, and Melissa pressed her hands to her mouth. She was wearing nothing but her bra and pants, and she knew it must seem as though Clifford had spent the night here.

'My God,' he went on, before she could speak, 'to think you almost had me believing in you. Half the time you act as though butter won't melt in your mouth. You even claim to have been let down so badly that you'll never let another man close. And then what do I find? That you've fed me a pack of lies, that you're actually sleeping with another man. And what galls me more is that you couldn't even wait until you got back to England.'

He was rocking on the balls of his feet by the time he had finished, his face an ugly red, his eyes glazed. He looked as though he'd had a sleepness night.

'No, Benedict, *no*. You have it all wrong.' Melissa's eyes were wide and pain-filled.

'Have I?' he demanded fiercely. 'Have I? I believe what my eyes tell me, and this is quite a pretty picture.' His gaze snaked over Melissa's half-naked body.

'Clifford didn't sleep here,' she protested. 'He's only just come.'

'Naturally,' he drawled. 'It's a good story, Melissa.

You stick to it—but don't expect me to believe it.'

The full force of his fury hit her as though it were a physical blow and she teetered backwards.

'If you won't believe Melissa then perhaps you'll believe me.' Clifford's tone was hard as he stepped forward to confront the other man. 'I did not sleep here. Check with reception if you want to verify that I have my own room.'

'What the hell difference does that make?' snarled Benedict. 'Who's to know which room you slept in?'

'I think too much of Melly to cheapen her in that way,' said Clifford coldly.

'Really?' sneered Benedict. 'You don't see a girl every single night of the week if there's nothing going on. What do you take me for, a fool?'

Melissa could stand no more. 'God, Benedict, what's wrong with you? If you can't accept that we're telling the truth then get out. I don't want to see you again if that's the way your mind works.'

He stared at her and then Clifford and then back again, breathing deeply, his eyes blazing, his fingers curled. 'Maybe I don't want to see you again either,' he muttered thickly.

'Good,' she crisped.

With one last condemning glare he strode out of the room and yet again Melissa collapsed into tears.

'Perhaps I ought to go and talk to him privately,' suggested Clifford, a worried frown deepening the creases on his brow. 'I can't bear to see you upset like this. Something has to be done about it.'

'It's no good going to him now,' choked Melissa. 'You'd probably end up fighting, and I should hate you to get hurt because of me.' She attempted to smile.

'Oh, I think I can stick up for myself,' said Clifford. 'I wasn't boxing champion at school for nothing. But you could be right, I might make matters worse for you. And I don't want to do that.' He looked at her thoughtfully 'What are you going to do, go back to England?'

'And risk being on the same flight as Benedict?' she protested. 'I don't think so.'

'You think he'll leave, too?'

She nodded. 'I'm sure of it.'

'Ah, well,' said Clifford cheerfully, 'we'll spend a few days unwinding. It's been years since I was in Paris.'

By the time she was dressed and ready to go out for breakfast—he had promised to take her to a little place he used to know overlooking the Seine—Melissa was feeling much better.

When yet another knock came on her door she sent a terrified glance in Clifford's direction. 'I bet it's Benedict,' she mouthed silently, moving across the room.

'Who is it?' she called without opening the door.

'It's me, I want to talk to you.'

She grimaced. 'There's nothing to discuss. You've made your point.'

'Melissa, open the door.'

'Just go away,' she said firmly.

'Melissa!' He sounded threatening.

She did not even answer. What on earth had made her fall in love with a man like this? Would she never learn?

He began to bang on the door and she thought he would break it down, or at the very least alert all the other guests on the same floor. But she was determined not to let him in. She wanted no more hassle, no more

unpleasant scenes. And in the end he did go. She heard
his door slam and shortly afterwards it opened and
slammed again. Loud footsteps sounded down the
corridor.

Her window overlooked the forecourt and several
minutes later she saw him climbing into a taxi, thrusting
his suitcase in before him.

'He's gone,' she said to Clifford, half sadly, half
relieved.

Melissa spent a pleasant couple of days in Clifford's
company. They took a leisurely cruise down the Seine,
watched the artists at work in the Place du Tertre, visited
the *Folies Bergère*, much to his enjoyment. He was a
marvellous companion, no one could have asked for
anyone better, and yet she could not get Benedict out of
her mind, no matter how she tried. Always he was
there—when she was asleep, when she was awake, when
she was relaxing alone, when she was with Clifford.

Benedict had hurt her deeply by his attitude. How
could he remain so adamant when they had both
protested their innocence? Didn't he want to believe her?
The more she thought about it the more confused she
became, and there were occasions when Clifford had to
snap her out of her melancholy.

'I think we ought to go home,' he said gently, on the
second evening. 'You're very good to me but your heart's
with Benedict, isn't it?'

She nodded, her eyes sad. 'I'm so hurt. How could he
accuse me of——'

'Shh.' He put his finger to her lips. 'Don't distress
yourself. I'll check on the flights. I think it might be a

good idea if we don't see so much of each other in future.'

'No!' Melissa shook her head fiercely. 'I need you, Cliff. You're the only person who really understands me.'

'You have Vivienne,' he reminded her gently.

'Vivienne's on Benedict's side,' claimed Melissa. 'She'll think I'm over-exaggerating.'

'We'll see.' He patted her hand and looked at her thoughtfully for several moments.

The instant Melissa walked into Vivienne's study the older woman demanded to know what had been happening.

'Benedict's furious. He says you're having an affair with Clifford. I didn't even know Clifford was in Paris.'

Melissa groaned inwardly. She had hardly slept for two nights, it had been a long and tiring day because the flight had been held up due to a bomb scare, and now all she wanted was the sanctity of her room, not to be put through a third degree about Benedict.

'Clifford came because I needed him. I was finding Benedict too much to handle,' she announced firmly. 'Do we have to discuss this now, Aunt Viv? I'm exhausted. I need to shower and freshen up before I can think or talk rationally.'

Vivienne eyed her frowningly, as though wondering whether this was an excuse, then she smiled and shrugged. 'Sorry, Melly, love. I hadn't noticed how tired you looked. Go on up to your room. We'll talk later.'

Meliss was almost out of the door when she remembered. 'I almost forgot. How's your ankle?'

Vivienne grimaced. 'Driving me nuts. I want to go to work but the damned doctor won't let me. Rest, he says.

Rest, rest, rest, unless I want recurring problems for the rest of my life.'

'Poor you.' Melissa knew how hard it must be for a woman as active as Vivienne.

'Don't pity me,' scoffed Vivienne. 'pity those around me. I've been like a bear with a sore head.'

'Maybe I should have stayed away,' grinned Melissa mischievously.

Vivienne held up her hand in a gesture of peace. 'I'll try not to get on to you, too.'

An hour later, refreshed and rested, Melissa went back downstairs. Vivienne's study was filled to overflowing with files but somehow she managed to make enough space to sit down.

'Now,' said Vivienne, 'what's this trouble with Benedict all about?'

Melissa explained and Vivienne listened patiently and then nodded. 'It sounds to me as though Benedict's fallen in love with you.'

'No!' She shook her head strongly. 'That's what Cliff says, but it's not true. Benedict and I will never, ever see eye to eye. We're totally incompatible.'

'Why else would he have reacted as he did when Clifford turned up?' Vivienne was not to be deterred. 'I sensed right from the beginning that he was interested in you. I was afraid, though, that he'd push you too much too soon. And I knew you weren't ready for any deep relationship. That's why I introduced you to Clifford. I thought he might help you come to terms with yourself. I thought be would be more understanding, having been widowed himself. But I never imagined it would have such explosive results.' She paused a moment, then said directly, 'Are you having an affair with Clifford?'

Melissa looked at her in exasperation. 'What do you think?'

Vivienne smiled ruefully and nodded. 'I'm sorry, I should have known better.'

'Precisely,' retorted Meliss tersely. She wondered whether everyone else was jumping to these same conclusions.

'So,' went on Vivienne with a sigh, 'what are we going to do about you and Benedict?'

'What do you mean, what are we going to do? There's nothing to be done. I don't want to see him again, it's as simple as that.'

Vivienne eyed her sadly. 'You're cutting off your nose to spite your face. You love him, don't you?'

Meliss groaned inwardly and nodded. 'Is it so obvious?'

'Only to those who care about you.'

'I still don't want to see him,' she protested. 'I didn't want it to happen, and I can't understand why it has. Why do I always attract the wrong men, Aunt Viv? Why can't I love Clifford? He's so understanding, so kind, so gentle.'

'Because,' answered Vivienne patiently, 'Clifford's learned the hard way. He's gone through all the heartache. I've no doubt he was once as easily upset or as quick to anger as Benedict, but time and pain are great mellowers.'

Melissa realised the wisdom behind her words. 'In that case I guess I'm destined to remain a spinster like you.'

'Oh, Melly love, no. Don't make my mistake.' Vivienne looked appalled. 'Life can be so lonely.'

'You could always marry Meredith.'

Vivienne nodded. 'Do you know something? That might not be a bad idea. But it's you we're discussing. I'm sure that Benedict loves you; why else would he be jealous of Clifford?

'I don't think it's jealousy,' said Melissa. 'I think his precious male ego's dented because I prefer Clifford's company, that's all. I bet there aren't many girls who've said "no" to Benedict.'

'I don't suppose there are,' admitted Vivienne. 'He's always been a charmer, right from when he was about ten years old. I've seen girls flocking around him like bees after honey. But I've never known him like this before. If he doesn't actually love you, Melly, then he's very strongly attracted.'

'You mean he wants to get me into bed?'

'That as well,' agreed the older woman with a smile. 'I imagine his male hormones work overtime whenever he looks at you, especially now you've come out of mourning.'

'Mourning?' Melissa's eyes widened dramatically. 'Is that what it looked like?'

'Worse. You looked dreadful. And if he fancied you then, well he must have it very bad.'

Melissa shook her head impatiently. 'You're talking about sex, of course.'

'No, dammit, I'm talking about love.' Vivienne's eyes sparked her anger. 'And I'm not going to sit back and let you two ruin your lives.'

'You're not?'

'No, I am not.'

Melissa smiled. 'So what are you going to do about it?'

'It's what you're going to do, my lady. You're going to stop playing games. For goodness' sake tell Benedict there's nothing between you and Clifford.'

'You think I haven't tried?'

'Then try harder. Stop seeing the man. Convince Benedict that you mean what you say.'

'Why should I?' demanded Melissa resentfully. 'Clifford's good for me.'

'He's served his purpose,' agreed Vivienne. 'And I think, Melly, love, it's now time to call it a day.'

'Well I don't,' snapped Melissa. 'I hope Clifford and I will always remain friends.'

Vivienne raised her hands in self-defence. 'Melly, I'm not suggesting you cut him dead, but I think you should reach a suitable compromise.'

Melissa felt deflated all of a sudden. 'Actually, Cliff himself suggested we see less of each other.'

They were silent for a second or two until Vivienne said. 'I want you to promise me something, Melly.'

Melissa eyed her suspiciously.

'I want you to promise that you'll try and be friends with Benedict.'

'Just like that?' scoffed Melissa. Heavens, what was Vivienne thinking? 'You've no idea how he riles me! Have a word with him, not me. He's the one who's at fault.'

Vivienne closed her eyes, shaking her head, lapsing again into silence.

Melissa did not like to see her unhappy. 'I suppose there's no harm in trying.' she said quietly, while secretly hoping that she would not see him again for a long time. It would never work. She just couldn't trust him. He wasn't the dependable type. Though had she questioned herself as to precisely why she had formed this opinion she would not have been able to find a satisfactory answer.

Vivienne beamed. 'Thank you, Melly. Now tell me, how did you enjoy the filming of the commercial? I've seen the rushes, they're marvellous. You must be feeling pretty pleased with yourself.'

'It was fantastic,' admitted Melissa enthusiastically, relieved to be talking about something other than Benedict. 'And I'm dying to see the film itself. Where's the next one going to be shot?'

They continued their discussion until it was time for dinner.

For the next few days Melissa worked at home and she enjoyed this because it meant she did not see Benedict. He spoke to Vivienne on the phone, and her pulses quickened whenever she heard his voice, but he had nothing to say to her, and for this she was grateful. It was the way she wanted it.

Though when she lay in bed at night it was impossible not to think about him. He was so near and yet so far. She sometimes thought she heard him moving about upstairs, and her heart would flutter, but she would quell it instantly. There could never, ever, be anything serious between her and Benedict. It just wouldn't work.

Then one evening he paid a call on them after dinner. Melissa could not control the frenzy of feelings that raced through her. Nothing had faded, none of the pulsing excitement caused by just looking at him, none of the instant desire. Nothing. He still managed to affect her as Tim never had.

Melissa was not so sure that Vivienne hadn't had a

hand in his being there, because although the other woman feigned surprise there was something in her expression that suggested she had known he was coming. And Melissa's suspicions were confirmed when Vivienne excused herself on the pretext of work after only a few minutes. Melissa's frantic silent appeal went unnoticed—or was it deliberately ignored?

She could not think of one word to say to him, and she wished herself anywhere but there. Vivienne was wrong in assuming they could sort things out. There was nothing to sort out. There was no future for them, not together.

There was a long, ominous silence in which she listened to the ticking of the clock, conscious of him looking at her, but unwilling to meet his gaze. It still amazed her that he had this power to render her helpless. She had never wanted to love again, not so soon, anyway, and she would have given anything, anything, just to get away from him now.

'So how's the great lover?'

Melissa jumped as his scathing tone broke the tension, and she finally looked at him. Everything went haywire after that. The blood pulsed through her veins and her heart raced. How she loved him, this man who was looking at her as though she were a stranger, as though nothing at all had ever passed between them; no intimacies, no kisses, no gentleness, no caring. His eyes were cold and condeming, and she wished with all her heart that she could hate him. She jutted out her chin. 'Clifford's fine.'

'I expected you to be out with him tonight.'

'Really?'

His lips tightened. 'Yes, really. Why aren't you?'

Her hackles began to rise. 'Not because I wouldn't like to be.' Then she remembered her vow to Viv, and in a slightly less agressive tone said, 'Actually I haven't seen him since we got back from Paris.'

His eyes narrowed. 'From choice?'

She lifted her shoulders. 'Partly. But mainly because I've been too busy.' She paused and looked at him, swallowing hard. This was going to be difficult. She wished she had never promised Vivienne. 'There really is nothing between us. He's a good friend to me, that's all. Can't you accept that? I needed someone.'

There was still tight anger on his face. 'Why him? Why not me? I tried.'

'You wanted too much from me, Benedict. I can relax with Clifford, knowing he will never want anything from me that I'm not prepared to give.'

He didn't believe her, it was there in his eyes.

'It's true,' she insisted.

'He spent the night with you,' he accused harshly.

'No, he didn't. Clifford's a gentleman. He's kind and thoughtful and considerate and he's never touched me, not in the way you're suggesting.'

'You're very convincing,' he managed after a while. 'Clifford's very lucky to have such a staunch supporter. But,' he added insolently, 'I'm really not interested.'

Melissa curled up inside and wished she had never opened her mouth. 'You make me sick, Benedict,' she raged. 'Clifford's worth ten of you. I wish I'd never promised Viv that I'd——' She stopped abruptly.

His brows rose. 'Go on. What was it that you promised?'

She closed her eyes for a second and took a good deep

breath. 'That I'd try and get on with you. Huh! Isn't that a laugh? It's a sheer impossibility. Vivienne obviously doesn't know you as well as she thinks she does.'

'On the contrary, Viv knows me only too well. But I'm intrigued. Why would she make you promise that?'

Melissa eyed him agressively. 'As if you don't know. She's playing matchmaker, isn't she. What a waste of time.'

'But you still decided to go along with her suggestion? Interesting.' He studied her face closely and Melissa wanted to look away but somehow couldn't. 'Why, I wonder, would Viv make such a suggestion? Have you given her any hint that you might be interested in me?'

She shrugged. 'Vivienne knows that I do feel a certain something for you.' She tried to make her tone nonchalant. 'It's just a perfectly normal reaction that any woman would have for an attractive man. But you and I both know there's nothing more to it than that. It's just a physical thing. She's making mountains out of molehills. It's ludicrous thinking that we'd ever fall in love.'

'Is it?' His dark eyes burned into hers.

'Of course. I've learned my lesson the hard way. No man is ever going to get the opportunity to hurt me again.'

He frowned. 'Why would a man who loves you want to hurt you?'

'You tell me that,' she cried. 'Tim always swore he loved me, he even had the gall to say he still loved me although he didn't want to marry me. Can you tell me how that is possible? Love and hurt go hand and hand as far as I'm concerned. Love makes you vulnerable. I'm never going to fall in love again.'

'I see.' His face was suddenly impassive, hiding whatever it was he felt at that moment. 'So Viv's hopes are never likely to be fulfilled?'

'Never,' she affirmed vehemently. 'Never! And I wish you'd tell her so.'

CHAPTER NINE

THE next morning, to Melissa's surprise, Vivienne decided she could be more profitably employed at the office, and it was even more of a shock when Benedict tapped on the door a few minutes later and announced that there was no point in them using two cars. 'You may as well come with me.' His smile was that of a cat who has stolen the cream.

Melissa fumed inwardly. It was a cut and dried arrangement, with no backing out. Obviously he and Vivienne had put their heads together last night. She felt like telling Viv where to stick her job, but that was no way to repay the woman's kindness. She would have to soldier along as best she could. Surely she was capable of handling Benedict, of being friends without letting emotions enter into it? Besides, she had made her point last night. If he was a gentleman he would keep his distance.

But it was not so easy for Melissa to keep that distance. Sitting in his car, breathing him, almost feeling him, her whole body a mass of sensation, evey nerve-end attuned, she could not ignore the love that burned within her. She was so afraid he might guess that she kept her head turned away, ostensibly watching the passing scenery, but in reality seeing nothing, her eyes blinded to everything except her feelings for this man beside her.

He did not speak. He turned on the radio and even

hummed a tune to himself. He was annoyingly cheerful.
Melissa glanced at him. His lips were curved in a smile
and she hungered to feel them on her own. She felt
starved of him, she realised. It was her own fault, she
consistently denied herself him, but that did not alter the
fact that she wanted to be taken into his arms and made
love to.

What was happening to her? What sort of a wanton
woman was she turning into? Oh, lord, it was going to be
hard working with him. She silently prayed that she
would be able to keep up the charade of indifference for as
long as it took.

He parked the black monster and they took the lift
together up to their floor. Melissa stood tall and still, eyes
to the front, wondering what would happen if the lift
broke down. They might be imprisoned here for hours!
Would he manage to keep his hands off her for that length
of time? Would she want him to? Would she turn to him
for comfort? For as long as she could remember Melissa
had always had a horror of being trapped in a lift, but
never had she imagined it would happen with a man that
she loved. It could make a world of difference.

She risked a glance at him. He was watching her, an
enigmatic expression in his eyes. Melissa had not realised
she was being scrutinised and her stomach muscles
tightened. She gave a tiny self-conscious smile.

'What are you thinking?'

She eyed him for second. 'I was just hoping the lift
wouldn't break down.'

No change came over his face but Melissa sensed a
tensing inside him. 'Because you would hate to be
trapped with me?'

'Something like that.' She shrugged.

'I'd be more interested in alerting someone to our plight than taking advantage of the situation.'

'And while we were waiting to be rescued?'

He grinned suddenly. 'You've obviously given the situation much thought. You tell me what you think I would do?'

Melissa groaned inwardly, wishing she had not been so honest. When the lift gave a sudden jolt her eyes widened and a moment's panic set in. It couldn't happen. No! And then the doors opened and a woman cleaner got in from one of the other floors.

Benedict's voice sounded softly in her ear. 'There's really no cause for such alarm. I promise I wouldn't rape you.'

Melissa looked anxiously to see whether the other woman had heard, but apparently not. She was busy watching the indicator and got off again on the next floor below theirs. And now there was not enough time for further conversation.'

When Benedict stopped to answer Tom Salmon's query as to how Vivienne was progressing, Melissa hurried along to her office alone. If this was an insight as to what the next few days were going to be like then they would be hell. And she had better pull herself together right now unless she wanted to make a complete fool of herself.

Actually, things went much more smoothly than Melissa expected, and in the days that followed she could not flaw Benedict's treatment of her. In fact he was too much of a gentleman. It was unlike him. She grew suspicious. Flowers began to arrive. He gave her a pair of mother-of-pearl combs for her hair, a pretty glass paperweight, a box of perfumed notepaper. What was all this? But whenever she questioned him or protested, he simply smiled and said why shouldn't he give a friend gifts?

And, since she had received presents from Clifford, Melissa had no grounds for argument.

He joined them for dinner most evenings, discussing the day's work with Vivienne, and the woman was clearly delighted at the harmony between him and Melissa.

Melissa was conscious of Benedict's eyes on her often, and always her insides began to melt, and she tried not to look at him. He was proving that he could be her friend, if that was all she would let him be. But the trouble was, she did not see him as a friend, not like Clifford. Her feelings for the two men were entirely different. And Benedict's goody-goody attitude was driving her insane.

It was such a relief when Vivienne announced one weekend that her doctor had pronounced her fit again and that she was going back to work on Monday. Now Melissa would not see so much of Benedict and she could get on with her life without him constantly disrupting it. She would never have let her mother ask Vivienne for a job if she had known she would be thrown into another man's company. It really was like being tossed out of the proverbial frying pan into the fire.

However, things got even worse when, on Sunday evening, Vivienne said, 'Well, Melly, love, I have a surprise for you.'

Melissa looked at her sharply and suspiciously, then stole a glance at Benedict who was standing a few feet away. His face was expressionless. Melissa did not know why she thought it might have something to do with him, she just did.

'Benedict's taking my place at an important presentation in London, and you're going with him.'

For a couple of seconds Melissa stood there stunned. 'Why?' she demanded at length.

'Because it's about time you got more involved in what goes on.'

'Have I any choice?' she asked mutinously.

Vivienne shook her head. 'It's all arranged.'

Melissa glared at Benedict, who suddenly grinned. 'You might surprise yourself, Melissa, and enjoy it.'

She lifted her shoulders, her expression saying that she had no intention of enjoying herself.

'You'll be leaving at half past six tomorrow,' announced Vivienne, 'so if I were you, Melly, I'd get your bag packed now and have an early night.'

Bag? What on earth was going on? 'Won't we be coming straight back?' She frowned.

This time Benedict answered her question. 'There are several other clients Vivienne wishes me to see while we're in London.'

It grew worse by the minute. 'So how long are we likely to be away?

He shrugged. 'Two or three days. It's hard to say.'

'And it doesn't really matter now I'm back in harness,' said Vivienne cheerfully. 'Besides, you deserve another break. You've worked hard these last few weeks.'

In other words, stay away as long as you like. Get to know Benedict, learn to trust him, show him you love him, come back and announce you're engaged. Melissa knew exactly the way Vivienne's mind worked.

Melissa could take no more. She bounced out of the room and upstairs, threw herself down on the bed, and

fumed. But it did no good, it altered nothing; she still had
to go with Benedict. It was part of her job.

Finally she managed to calm herself sufficiently to
throw some clothes into a case and take a shower. Then
she went to bed.

When her alarm woke her at a quarter to six Melissa
leapt out of bed, washed and dressed in a grey linen suit
and a crisp white blouse, applied make-up, pinned back
her hair at the sides with the combs he had bought, and
found Benedict downstairs waiting for her.

She gave him a warily cheerful, 'Good morning.' If
they were going to be thrust into each other's company for
the next few days there was no sense in being at
loggerheads.

His gaze flickered over her. 'Very smart, but not how I
like to see you.'

She knew he preferred her to wear pretty clothes that
showed off her figure and femininity. 'I've not dressed to
please you,' she said. 'I'm representing your company,
aren't I?'

He inclined his head. 'Of course.'

They left the house before Vivienne had even got up
but, whereas Melissa had expected him to drive up to
London, instead they took a taxi to the railway station
and went by train. She actually found this preferable. The
train was full and there was none of the intimacy she had
dreaded on the long journey by car.

Benedict purchased a newspaper for himself and a
magazine for Melissa from the station bookshop, and they
spent almost the whole of the journey reading.

The day passed quickly after that. The presentation
was a complete success, their client perfectly happy with

their suggestions, and when they reached their hotel that evening Melissa felt pretty pleased with the way the day had gone.

Now that she was learning more about the company and the way they did things she was able to take an active part in the discussion, and she had felt inordinately pleased when once or twice Benedict had asked her opinion.

'Where are we going tomorrow?' she asked over dinner. She had changed out of her business suit into a jersey silk oatmeal dress that moulded itself to her figure. She wore it with her conker-coloured belt and shoes, and had left her hair loose. The success of the day had added a sparkle to her eyes and there was a glow about her of which she was ignorant.

But Benedict did not miss one tiny thing. His eyes appraised every inch of her, and if for once they revealed more than he wished, Melissa did not notice. He had praised her today and she felt warm and good and completely attuned to him. She had forgotten her animosity. They were business colleagues, nothing more.

'We have one call in the morning at Ellis and Brunel, and then our day is free.'

'And the day after?' She wondered exactly how long they would be here.

'It all depends. I have a phone call to make first. But does it matter? I thought we might take in a couple of shows. Make the most of it. I know Vivienne won't mind.'

Melissa had never been to a London theatre, and to her own surprise she found herself nodding enthusiastically. 'I'd like that.'

The next night they went to see *The Mouse Trap* and the night after that they saw *Cats,* and in all that time

Benedict never once kissed her. She could not believe it. Had he accepted that she wanted nothing more than friendship? Had he given up trying to seduce her?

Ironically she found herself wanting him more and more. There was a kind of desperation inside her as she willed him to kiss her, to see her as a sexually desirable woman and not as Vivienne's personal assistant learning the trade. It was a complete reversal of her initial attitude towards him. It was madness.

But when the next day he hired a car instead of taking the usual taxi, and when he drove several miles outside London towards Colchester, turning off the main road and negotiating several turnings until he finally stopped at an imposing white house on the outskirts of Coggeshall, she felt suddenly uneasy.

'Where are we?'

He smiled disarmingly. 'My parents' home.'

Melissa could not hide her horror. 'Why?'

'I thought they might like to meet you.'

'Meet me? Why would they want to meet me? What have you told them? Benedict. *Benedict!*'

He was climbing out of the car, ignoring her questions, smiling blithely as he waited for her to follow him up the path.

Melissa could not imagine what he was up to, and her steps were hesitant before he took her hand and pulled her along with him. Was this part and parcel of what he and Vivienne had planned? She felt dreadful. What a devious trick to play on anyone. She wasn't even prepared. Did she look all right? Was her skirt creased? Was her hair tidy? Had she any lipstick left on? Damn Benedict! How dared he do this to her?

But several minutes later she was damning him even more strongly. The door opened as they approached it; they were obviously expected. His mother was tall and elegant with blue-rinsed hair, a strong face and Benedict's eyes. She looked as though she would stand no nonsense.

Benedict hugged her and kissed her and then turned to Melissa. 'Mother, meet Melissa, the girl I'm going to marry.'

Shockwave after shockwave rippled through Melissa. What sort of a sick joke was this? If it had been a novel she was reading this would be the end of the chapter. A cliff-hanger. She would have been eager to read on to see what was going to happen next. But this was no story; this was real life, and she didn't want to know. She wanted to turn round and leave; she wanted to go back to Vivienne. No, not even there. She wanted to go home, to her mother. Vivienne had conspired with Benedict. It was a heinous plot, and Melissa felt devastated.

'Melly, my mother, Mrs Cameron.'

'Melissa.' The woman held out an elegant hand. 'How nice to meet you.' But she did not sound pleased, and the way Mrs Cameron looked her up and down made Melissa feel as though she was being inspected and found wanting.

Mrs Cameron's hand was cold and she barely touched Melissa's fingers before withdrawing. 'Do come in, both of you.'

Melissa tried to attract Benedict's attention, clutching at his arm, attempting to stop him, but he merely patted her hand and forged on behind his mother.

Benedict's stepfather, tall and grey-haired, was a much milder man, and he smiled with genuine warmth as he was introduced to Melissa. She liked him much better.

'Would you like a drink? A sherry perhaps?' Although I do think you might have warned us, Benedict. This is a complete surprise.'

'I rang you and said I was coming.'

'But not that you were bringing—a girl with you. Who is she, Benedict? Why haven't you told us about her before?

Melissa felt both embarrassed and furious at being spoken about in this manner.

'Oh, come on, Mother,' said Benedict. 'You know you're never interested.'

'And what has this one got that Felicity hasn't?'

He had his back to Melissa but she saw the sudden tensing of his shoulders. 'Surely that's obvious.' He turned to Melissa and smiled. 'What would you like to drink?'

Her eyes darkened and there was not even a hint of a returning smile on her lips. 'A cup of tea, please.' Who was this Felicity? An old flame? Someone of whom his mother approved? Heavens, she was welcome of him.

Mrs Cameron's finely plucked brows rose. Melissa could read her mind. Tea? How absurd.

'A good idea,' said Benedict before his mother could speak. 'We'll drink that toast later.'

Never, if she had anything to do with it, decided Melissa, impatient to speak privately with Benedict. What a nerve. What a cheek! How dared he? And, more to the point, why hadn't she contradicted him? Why had she meekly stood and let his mother think it was the truth?

Surely she hadn't been frightened of causing a scene? What would it matter? She did not know these people; she was not likely to meet them again. It was insanity saying he was going to marry her. What did he mean by it? Not one word of love had ever passed his lips, and he had absolutely no idea how she felt about him. Had he? Vivienne wouldn't have said anything. The thought made her go hot all over. What if she had? What if she had told him? Oh, lord!

But that was still no reason for him to tell his parents that she was the girl he was going to marry. His interest in her was purely sexual, she felt certain. It was an absolute mystery why he had made that strange statement.

'Melly.'

Melissa suddenly realised that Benedict was speaking to her.

'Where were you, Melly?'

As if he didn't know. 'I'm sorry, what did you say?'

'David just asked how you were enjoying working for us?'

'I love it,' she said, flashing the older man a smile. 'I find it extremely interesting.'

'And Benedict tells me you're full of good ideas?'

She shrugged. 'I've had one or two. But none as brilliant as Benedict's.' Like telling a girl you were going to marry her when it was the last thing she expected, or wanted! She glared at him, not caring that the other man was watching.

'He's had a lifetime's experience.'

Of seducing women! 'I'm sure he has,' she said sweetly. And, to Benedict, 'Do you always get the results you hope for?'

His lips quirked. 'Without fail. I'll go and see if my mother needs a hand.'

'Do sit down,' said David Cameron. 'I must admit Benedict's dropped quite a bombshell. We had no idea there was any girl he was serious about.'

Melissa gave a weak smile and said nothing. What could she say? Tell David it was all a huge joke? Obviously Benedict had some reason for saying what he had and she would eventually discover what it was. Meanwhile all she could do was go along with the delusion.

'He says you've only been with the firm for a few weeks. I always guessed when Benedict finally fell in love it would be a sudden affair. Patricia will be pleased. She wants him to get married.' He seemed not to have noticed his wife's coldness towards her.

'What do you do for a living, Mr Cameron? she asked, desperately seeking a change of topic.

'I'm a retired police inspector,' he said.

Her eyes widened. 'That must have been interesting.'

'It was,' he admitted. 'I miss it.'

'And what do you do now to keep occupied?'

He went on to tell her about the various hobbies he had, and then Benedict and his mother returned.

Patricia poured the tea into dainty china cups and handed round a plate of fancy biscuits. 'I was just saying to Benedict that we can't let this occasion pass without a celebration.'

'And so,' continued Benedict, 'my mother's going to throw a party for us tomorrow night.'

'You mean we're staying here?' asked Melissa in horror.

He nodded, smiling pleasantly. 'That's right, darling.'

'But my work, and Vivienne. Isn't she expecting us

back?' How dared her 'darling' her!

'I'll give her a ring and explain,' he said airily.

She clenched her teeth. Things were going too far. 'I'd like a word with you, Benedict, alone,' she whispered fiercely.

He was completely unperturbed. 'All in good time. Drink your tea first. Although I think I know what it is you want to say, what all you girls say on these sort of occasions. You haven't anything suitable to wear. Isn't that it? Never mind, we'll go shopping tomorrow. We can't have an engagement party without a ring, can we?'

Melissa was dumbfounded. This really was carrying things too far. Angrily she stood up. 'I want to speak to you now.'

She did not care that Patricia was frowning at her display of bad manners, that David looked mildly surprised. They had to sort this thing out without delay. She ought to have spoken her mind right from the beginning.

Benedict patted her arm indulgently. 'Just as you wish, Melly. I'm sorry, Mother, David, if you'll excuse us.'

He took Melissa's elbow and led her from the room. At the bottom of the stairs she rounded on him heatedly.

'What the hell do you think you're playing at? How dare you tell your parents that we're getting married? I've never heard anything so absurd in all my life.'

He took her shoulders and looked at her, his face quite serious. 'I don't think it's ridiculous, Melly.'

'Of course it is,' she snapped, backing away from him, not really taking in what he had said. 'I felt like a complete fool. Why did you do it?'

'Because I want to marry you.'

Melissa's heart began to bang painfully against her ribcage. 'That's nonsense. Why?'

He smiled. 'Why does a man usually want to marry a woman? I think you'd make me a very good wife.'

Melissa had the sudden insane notion that he might have said he loved her. What a pathetic thought. She eyed him crossly. 'You'd marry me even though I don't love you?'

'That would come, in time,' he said confidently. 'We're compatible physically; that will do for a start.'

'And that's all you think about, isn't it?' she demanded, 'My God, I've heard some stories but this takes the biscuit. You'd go so far as to marry me just to get me into bed. I can't believe it.'

'I didn't say that,' he said quietly. 'If you don't want sex I shan't force you. I know you still have a long way to go before you get over what Tim did to you. I want to prove that I'm not like him, that you can trust me, that I shall never, ever let you down.'

Her green eyes flashed. 'You mean you want to prove that you'll marry me even though he wouldn't. What sort of a bizarre idea is that, Benedict? I don't understand. I really don't.'

'Maybe I shouldn't have sprung it on you,' he smiled. 'But is the idea so abhorrent?'

Melissa closed her eyes. It wasn't. Of course it wasn't. She loved him, and the thought of being his wife was really quite exciting. Had he said he loved her she might even have entertained it, despite her earlier vows to remain single. But it wouldn't work. A one-sided love affair was no good to anyone. He would tire of her eventually, as Tim had done. And a divorce would be even more harrowing than what she had already gone through.

'Well, Melissa?'

She looked at him, realising he was still waiting for her answer. 'It's out of the question.'

His lips firmed. 'I have no intention of going back in there and telling my mother that it's off. Will it really do any harm, Melissa, getting engaged to me? We don't have to get married straight away. Who knows, you might find you quite like the idea, and if you don't, after a reasonable period, then I'll give in gracefully.'

What could she say? She still could not begin to understand why, but it would be easier to go through with the charade, for a few days at least. She lifted her shoulders helplessly. 'You win.'

He grinned and pulled her against him, and Melissa felt a sudden warmth steal through her. Whether she liked it or not, it felt good in his arms.

'I'll show you where you're going to sleep,' he said, letting her go abruptly.

Melissa felt disappointed that he had not kissed her. Wasn't it what a truly loving man would have done? But he didn't love her, did he? It was some strange and foolish game he was playing. And what was the point in one kiss if he could not follow it up with more satisfying lovemaking?

Her lips clamped together as she followed him up the stairs. It was quite a large house and the room he took her to was right at the end of a long landing. But it was a pretty room nevertheless, decorated in sunshine yellow with its own tiny shower-room en suite, and a window overlooking the beautifully landscaped gardens at the back of the house.

'Thank you,' she said, 'I'll be down in a minute. Would you mind getting my case out of the car?'

'For my beloved, anything,' he smiled with a mock bow. 'But your tea is getting cold. Won't your unpacking wait until later?'

Melissa did not want to face his parents again, not yet, not until she had grown more accustomed to acting the part of Benedict's fiancée. But, short of another argument, what choice had she?

'I suppose so,' She shrugged, and followed him back out. 'Which is your room?'

He turned and grinned. 'Thinking of coming in to me in the middle of the night?'

Melissa did not find it funny. 'Like hell I will. I shall keep my door locked and bolted.'

He grew serious all of a sudden. 'You have nothing to fear from me, Melissa, you should know that. I'm sure I've never given you any reason to believe such a thing.'

She felt a bit silly. 'No, you haven't. I'm sorry, I'm all on edge.'

'Poor Melly,' he mocked. 'I really have thrown you in at the deep end, haven't I?' He pulled her to him, holding her close for a second, feeling the tenseness within her.

His hand stroked her hair and he felt so strong and warm and comforting that slowly Melissa relaxed and feelings of an entirely different kind began to grow inside her.

It seemed so long since the last time he had kissed her. When was it? In Paris? Oh, how much she wanted him to kiss her now. She needed the strength of him to seep into her. She needed his courage, his love.

No, not love. She shook her head. He would never love her. That was a fool's dream.

'What is it, my Melly?' Her action had not gone unnoticed.

She lifted her head to look at him, her eyes full of wonder. His tone had been soft, warm, possessive. Not as though he was acting a part. My Melly. A thrill rode through her. How she would love to be his Melly, for all time. It was a surprising realisation, and an impossibility, she knew, but perhaps it might help her to get through this next day or two.

Their eyes met and he did not wait for her answer. With a groan he lowered his head, his mouth hungrily covering hers. Melissa's lips parted as she felt the flood of desire well up inside her. Of their own volition her hands went around him and she responded with a mutually deep thirst.

How long the kiss went on she had no idea. It seemed like forever, his mouth moving from her lips to her throat and her ears, nuzzling, biting, thrilling, his hands feeling her, moulding her, creating whole new sensations, and when he finally tried to gently put her from him she did not want to let go.

He touched her chin with his finger. 'You needed that?'

She nodded.

'Me, too.' His eyes were dark with passion. 'Whatever else our relationship lacks, it's not this, is it?'

Melissa mutely shook her head, conscious that her eyes must be shining, her cheeks warm with colour, her lips soft. She hoped she wasn't giving too much away. But she could not help it. He had resurrected feelings she had tried desperately hard to keep in check. There was no way at that moment that she could hide them.

They walked back into his parents' drawing-room hand in hand. David smiled, but there was a faint frown on Patricia's brow. It failed, however, to penetrate Melissa's temporary euphoria and she sat down and picked up her cup as though nothing at all had happened.

It was obvious from her expression that the older woman was dying to know why Melissa had wanted to speak to Benedict, but he did not give her the satisfaction of an explanation, merely briefly apologising for their absence and then recounting an amusing tale of a commercial that had gone wrong.

Afterwards he went out to his car to fetch in their cases while David took Melissa to see his garden and Patricia returned to the kitchen to organise lunch.

The day passed uncomfortably slowly, Melissa only too well aware of Patricia's disapproval. It amazed her that Benedict seemed oblivious to his mother's attitude.

Once dinner was over Benedict suggested they go for a walk.

'I'd love to,' answered Melissa at once. Anything to get away from his mother, who had been going on all through dinner as to who would or would not be coming to the party.

Apparently, while they were out in the garden, Patricia phoned around telling everyone about Benedict's engagement, and just about the whole neighbourhood was going to be there, plus all sorts of other friends and relations as well.

'I don't think I can stand this,' said Melissa. 'It sounds

like I'm going on show.'

He smiled. 'Mother's enjoying herself. She loves organising.'

'But you're going to feel such a fool when it's all over, the engagement, I mean. What will you say? That I wasn't suitable after all?'

He put an arm about her shoulders and hugged her to him. 'I don't think the problem will arise.'

She looked at him scathingly. 'It will.'

The next day they went out to buy her a new dress and the ring. Benedict chose both; Melissa had no interest in the matter. She simply couldn't understand what game he was playing.

But she could not deny that the ring was gorgeous, and expensive. It was a six-tier cluster ring with a hundred diamonds in it, and she could hardly believe that he would pay so much. It felt heavy on her finger and she kept looking at it, and twisting it, and wishing the whole affair was for real.

She wished that Benedict did love her, and he did want to marry her. She had thought about it a lot in bed last night and had finally reached the decision that she was not destined to be an old maid. She did want to get married one day. Tim hadn't been the right man, it was as simple as that. But Benedict was. If only he loved her, too.

CHAPTER TEN

THE guests began to arrive and Melissa was introduced to so many people that she knew she would never remember their names, or whether they were relatives or friends, or anything at all about them. Benedict remained at her side, his arm around her waist, the devoted bridegroom-to-be.

It was one of those balmy summer evenings, so infrequent in England, when it was possible to entertain outdoors, and coloured lights had been strung through the trees ready for when it grew dusk. On the patio were tables and chairs, with chilled punch, nuts and savoury biscuits and various dips. Later there would be an elaborate buffet supper, as well as champagne for the toast to the happy couple. David had cleverly wired up some speakers and soft music filled the air.

Patricia Cameron had gone to so much trouble that Melissa felt embarrassed. It was all for nothing. How could Benedict let his mother do it? But she dutifully smiled and accepted congratulations and was glad that she had let Benedict buy her a new dress. Nothing she had brought with her would have compared with the creations that were being aired here tonight. It was like a gala ball given in honour of some very important person. Did Benedict's mother always entertain so lavishly?

When all the guests had arrived Melissa and Benedict

began to mingle. She felt good in her long oyster silk dress which was deceptively simple and had been horrendously expensive. It made her look even taller and quite slender and elegant. In her ears were the diamond studs Benedict had given to her earlier as an engagement present.

He had come to her bedroom as she was giving herself a last-minute inspection. Standing behind her, meeting her eyes through the mirror, he had lifted her hair to one side and kissed her nape, sending shivers down Melissa's spine, and handed her the gift.

'Oh, Benedict, don't you think you've given me enough?' She had turned round to face him, her green eyes troubled. 'I can't accept any more, I really can't.'

'It's not much, just a little trinket to complete the picture. You're so beautiful, my Melly. So lovely. I'm very proud of you.'

'But it's all in vain,' she whispered. 'I feel such a fraud.'

'It's not in vain,' he had said gravely, his hands cupping her face, his thumb touching her lower lip, pulling it gently down so that he could kiss the soft moistness within. 'I meant what I said about wanting to marry you.' His breath had been warm against her cheek. 'And I don't intend taking no for an answer.'

Melissa had closed her eyes, feeling a delicious thrill course through her. But what nonsense he was speaking. It was a game, nothing more. Wasn't it? He couldn't force her to marry him. But she could feel the warmth of him, his sensuality, his desire. He looked so handsome and distinguished in his white dinner jacket. She loved him so much.

Suddenly she had wanted to run away, just the two of

them, to escape all this fuss. She had wanted to go miles away, to a desert island if necessary, so that she could get to know Benedict, really know him.

His thoughts ran deep; she wanted to probe them. She wanted to know the way his mind worked, his feelings, his desires. Why he was doing this to her.

He was an extremely sexy man; she wanted to find about about that side of him as well. Her own sexuality was not yet fully awakened, he had proved that already, but he could do it, and she wanted to experience the thrill and satisfaction of that side of such a relationship.

But she had said none of this to Benedict, merely pulling away from him and smiling weakly. 'You know how I feel, Benedict. There's no point in going through it all again.'

She had accepted the earrings, though, and she felt like a million dollars as she walked with him now through the garden.

'You do realise that I'm the envy of every man here tonight?' he said softly in her ear.

Melissa smiled up at him. He was making a very good job of pretending that she meant everything to him, and like a fool she was basking in it, responding, even imagining that he did actually love her.

Melissa became aware all of a sudden that several pairs of eyes had turned towards the house. She stopped and looked, too, and felt Benedict stiffen. One last guest had made her appearance. And what an appearance.

Her thick black hair curled to her shoulders and framed her face. Her eyes were dark and wide, her lashes thick and long. Her diamond earrings fell almost to her shoulders. Her dress of ice-blue jersey lurex was long-sleeved and close-fitting, the long skirt split at the side to mid-thigh, and the front cut in a V almost to her waist.

It was sensational, and the girl knew it. She stood there like a film star, her eyes searching the assembled guests, finally alighting on Benedict.

'Ah, there you are,' she seemed to say, and with her arm outstretched she moved unerringly towards him, the other people stepping to one side to form a pathway for her.

Melissa looked at Benedict. He was frowning. 'Who is that?' she whispered. But he did not hear. His attention was totally taken up by this beautiful latecomer.

And suddenly Melissa knew. Some sixth sense told her that this was the mysterious Felicity. She searched the crowd for Mrs Cameron and spotted her not many yards away. Her thin lips were smiling, her eyes watching the other girl's progress with satisfaction. Most probably she had herself asked Felicity to make this dramatic entrance, thought Melissa.

She turned again to watch the beautiful black-haired girl striding confidently towards them. The raspberry-red lips were curved into an alluring smile, teeth white and even, her eyes on Benedict alone.

'Darling,' she purred. 'It's been so long, too long.' Her hand touched his arm possessively and, ignoring Melissa, she turned her face up for a kiss.

Melissa felt sickened and would have walked away had Benedict's mother not appeared at their side. 'Felicity, dear, how nice you could make it.'

As if she hadn't stage-managed the whole affair! It was perfectly clear that his mother would prefer him to marry Felicity. But what were his feelings? He certainly looked as though he was enjoying the kiss.

They broke apart when his mother spoke, and the girl smiled warmly at Mrs Cameron. 'I wouldn't have missed this for the world.' Then her eyes swivelled to Melissa and there was nothing in them except ice-cold hatred. 'Benedict, darling, aren't you going to introduce us?'

Benedict put his arm about Melissa's shoulders, holding her against him, smiling gently. If Melissa had not know better she would have sworn there was a look of love in his eyes.

'Felicity, meet my fiancée, Melissa Sutherland. Melly, Felicity Howes, a family friend.'

'A very close family friend,' confirmed his mother.

Melissa automatically held out her hand but the other girl's response was perfunctory, no more.

'This is a surprise, Benedict.' Felicity looked again at him. 'When your mother phoned me I nearly dropped through the floor.'

'I'm sure it is,' he said. 'Aren't you going to offer us your congratulations?'

The girl's eyes narrowed spitefully. 'But of course. I hope you'll both be very happy. Have you told Melissa about us, darling? About how close we once came to getting married ourselves?'

Melissa felt his arm tighten about her. 'No, I haven't, Felicity. It's hardly the thing to talk about to your future wife. I'm sure Melissa has no interest in any of my past girlfriends.'

'Oh, my dear, you're wrong. We girls love to know these things. Hasn't she asked you? Isn't she curious? I mean, you're thirty-five. You're hardly likely to be pure.' She gave a brittle laugh. 'Melissa, I could tell you enough about Benedict to make your toes curl. He's a gorgeous hunk, isn't he? I'm sure I don't know how you managed to trap him. Heaven knows I've tried hard enough myself.'

'Perhaps you tried too hard,' said Benedict coolly. 'If you'll excuse us, we really must mingle.'

'I'll see you later, darling.' Felicity trailed her fingers down Benedict's arm. 'I want to talk to you—alone.'

She spoke softly but Melissa heard, probably she was intended to, and she found it difficult to return Benedict's smile as he led her away.

'Ignore Felicity,' he said. 'She just likes to cause trouble.'

'You were in love with her once?'

'I thought I was, yes, but that was many years ago. We had an affair. It didn't last. It taught me a thing or two about her that I hadn't known. She's terribly possessive for one thing, and I don't like that in a woman.'

'You like your freedom too much? I somehow don't think you'll ever get married.'

'Melissa!' He stopped dead in his tracks and looked at her. 'What sort of a remark is that from my fiancée?'

'Oh, come on,' she protested, trying to laugh, 'we both know this isn't for real.'

'Isn't it?' he asked quietly.

'I don't love you,' she lied.

His lips firmed. 'You'll learn.'

When Mrs Cameron announced that supper was ready there was a general surge towards the buffet table, and Melissa took the opportunity to go into the house for a moment's peace and quiet.

It had been quite a strain talking to so many different

people, trying to pretend a happiness she was far from feeling. Had it been a genuine engagement, if Benedict had loved her as she did him, then she would have been ecstatic, and it would have shown, and every single person here would have felt envious. But that wasn't to be. They were playing Benedict's game. Something to do with his mother, she imagined. She was quite convinced he had no intention of actually marrying her, even though he kept saying so. Perhaps Mrs Cameron was always harping on about him getting married and it was all for her benefit. Whatever, the whole thing was giving her a headache, and if she didn't get away for a while she would scream.

But Melissa's wish for solitude was not to be. Felicity followed her into the house, her face now an evil mask of fury. 'At last. I've been waiting for an opportunity to have a private word.'

Melissa eyed her coldly, her brows arched. She said nothing.

'Benedict won't marry you.'

'Really?' asked Melissa. She could have told her that.

'He's not the marrying type. We were engaged once. The poor darling doesn't know what he wants.'

'And you do, I suppose?' This woman annoyed her.

Felicity's smile held no warmth; it was more like a sneer. 'I think I can safely say I know what Benedict wants better than he does himself. It's only a matter of time, Melissa, before we get back together. Your engagement was a bit of a shock, I must admit. But it just means that I'll have to work on him sooner that I'd planned.'

She sounded so confident. Obviously she had no idea

that Benedict no longer felt anything for her, that she had killed any feelings he had by her possessiveness.

'You really think he'll come back to you?'

'Of course. There's no question about it. Benedict and I have known each other for years. Everyone here is as shocked as I am. It was a foregone conclusion that we'd sort out our differences and get married eventually. I think we're made for each other.'

Heaven help him, thought Melissa, if this woman really did get her talons into him again. She was a prize bitch. 'We'll have to wait and see, won't we?' she said, smiling sweetly.

'I just thought you needed telling what you're up against.'

Melissa met the spiteful dark eyes. 'I think I can handle it.'

'You sound very confident.'

'And why shouldn't I be? I'm the one wearing his ring.' She flaunted it beneath Felicity's nose. 'Isn't it beautiful? It cost the earth. Wouldn't you say he loves me a lot to buy me something like this?'

Felicity tossed her head angrily. 'He loved me, too, once, and I'm damn well going to make sure that he loves me again.' With one last vengeful glare she turned and left the house.

Melissa closed her eyes and groped for the nearest chair. She could have done without that. After a few seconds' controlled breathing she felt better. What a prime statement that had been—Benedict loved her. But at least it had done the trick. It had got rid of Felicity Howes.

She remained there several minutes longer and was

about to push herself up and rejoin the others when Benedict came looking for her.

He frowned when he saw her pale face. 'Melly, love, is something wrong?'

She grimaced. 'I have a headache.' Which was the truth.

'Have you taken anything for it?'

Melissa shook her head.

'I'll fetch you some aspirin.'

He was back in less than a minute and stood over her as she swallowed them down, taking the water glass away, and then sitting beside her.

'Is all this a bit too much for you?'

'What do you think?'

'I never expected my mother to go this far, I must admit.'

'It's madness,' said Melissa.

'She loves it.'

'And David?'

Benedict grinned. 'He keeps out of the way.

'I thought I hadn't seen him. He's a wise man. Does your mother throw parties often?'

'Whenever she can find an excuse. But she's excelled herself this time. How are you feeling now? Shall we go and join the others? I don't know about you but I'm ravenous.'

So they went back outside and ate supper, and a toast was drunk to them, and Benedict looked supremely happy. It was growing dusk; the lights were switched on and everywhere had a fairytale magic about it.

Some of the couples began dancing. Benedict pulled Melissa into his arms, and she let herself dream. Held close against him, feeling the warmth of his body, his total maleness, closing her eyes to the fact that their engagement was no more than a game, she imagined that it was all for real. That he loved her as deeply as she loved him, and soon they would be married, and they would spend the rest of their lives together.

But all too soon Benedict was claimed by Felicity, and he could not ignore her. They were split up and Melissa found herself dancing with one man after another; she could not see Benedict.

When she did eventually spot him he was still dancing with Felicity, her arms entwined around his neck, his arms around her, his hands so low on her back that it made Melissa grow hot. Felicity's lips were invitingly close to his. She was blatantly offering herself to him, and he looked as though he was enjoying every minute of it.

Jealousy seared through Melissa. It should not matter. He was entitled to kiss whomever he liked. But couldn't he have waited until after the party? Didn't he know that everyone was looking at them? Or was he oblivious to everyone else? Had he not been speaking the truth when he said he no longer loved Felicity? Now she was in his arms, did everyone else fade into oblivion? It was certainly what it looked like.

Melissa turned her head away, but in doing so caught sight of Mrs Cameron watching her. There was a smile of triumph on the woman's face. This was what she had planned all along. This wasn't a party to celebrate their engagement, it was a party to ruin it. The other guests were all foils. Felicity was the central character. And it was all going according to plan.

Finally people began drifting away. Benedict returned

to Melissa's side, and together with his parents they said goodbye to everyone and wished them a safe journey home. Until at last there was only Felicity left.

She turned one of her practised smiles on Benedict. 'Call me a taxi, there's a darling. I really shall have to find myself another man. It's such a bore having to travel everywhere alone.'

'I'll run you home,' he said, as she had known he would.

'Don't be long,' said his mother, 'or you'll make Melissa jealous.'

He glanced fondly at her. 'Melly knows there's no need for that, don't you, my love?'

Melissa's throat was contracted so tightly she could not speak. She simply smiled and nodded and waited for the moment she could go up to her room.

As soon as Benedict left with Felicity they all three walked into the house. David looked relieved, Patricia Cameron very satisfied, and Melissa felt ready to cry. What on earth was happening to her life? She had asked for none of this; she had been so careful not to get involved again, and yet look what a mess she was in.

David poured himself a large Scotch and sank down into an armchair. 'Thank goodness that's over. What are you, Patricia, a masochist?'

'I think it went down very well,' she said, 'considering the short notice I had. What do you think, Melissa?'

Melissa shrugged but an innate politeness would not let her be rude. 'It was a delightful party. Thank you. Would you excuse me if I go to bed now? I'm very tired.

'Of course, my dear.' Patricia Cameron gave a gracious smile.

But Melissa had been in bed for no more than ten minutes when the woman came into her room. 'I'd like a few words with you, while Benedict's out of the way.'

Melissa eyed her suspiciously. Now what? Hadn't she suffered enough this evening? Hadn't Patricia's little ploy worked without her needing to rub salt into the wounds?

'I won't beat around the bush. This has to be said.' Mrs Cameron's eyes were hard. 'It has always been my wish for Benedict to marry Felicity. I was distraught when they split up. But I still believe that they are right for each other, and I——'

'I'm sorry, Mrs Cameron.' Melissa could not let her go on. 'I think that what Benedict does with his life has nothing at all to do with you. If he'd wanted to marry Felicity he would have done so.'

'Felicity was young and foolish,' insisted the older woman. 'She messed up her chances. She's a different person now, and she loves Benedict—which is more than I think you do.'

Melissa gasped. At least she could be truthful on this one. 'Oh, no, Mrs Cameron, you have that all wrong. I love your son very much.'

'You didn't look happy when Benedict announced your engagement.' said Patricia Cameron grimly. 'I think I can rightly say it was as much a surprise to you as it was to me. I know my son, Melissa, and it is my belief that the only reason he suggested getting engaged was to safeguard himself from Felicity.'

'That's ridiculous,' snapped Melissa. 'Why would he need to do that? Is he afraid of her?'

'Felicity's a very—how shall I put it?—a very determined woman. And no man likes to be chased. But the truth of the matter is that he does love Felicity. He's simply not giving himself the chance to realise it. You saw them together tonight. They disappeared for over an house. Is that the behaviour of a man happily contemplating marriage? I think you have to face it, Melissa, that when he comes back he'll have changed his mind about you. I'm sorry to be so pessimistic, but——'

'I bet you are.' Melissa could contain her temper no longer. 'You planned all this, didn't you? You invited Felicity deliberately. You hated me on sight. OK, I'll be frank. I have no intention of marrying Benedict. But he doesn't love Felicity, and he'll never marry her in a hundred years.'

She paused and drew breath. 'He told me exactly how he feels about her, and I believe him. I suggest, Mrs Cameron, that you let your son get on with his own life and stop interfering.'

The woman gasped, but Melissa went on, 'Is the reason he's still single because you've treated every one of the girlfriends he's brought here the way you have me? Have you frightened them all away? Has Felicity been brought on to the scene every single time? I'm sorry, Mrs Cameron, if I'm speaking out of place, but that's the way

I feel, and I feel sorry for Benedict having a mother like you. Can I use your phone please? I'd like to call a taxi. I'm going home.' And to hell with the cost!

CHAPTER ELEVEN

MELISSA swung her legs over the edge of the bed, pushing her arms in to her robe as she rushed from the room—all before Mrs Cameron could say another word—and ran full tilt into Benedict.

She had not realised he was back and wondered how much he had heard. He caught her arms and steadied her. 'What the hell's going on?' A deep frown was carved on his brow.

Words would not come; she was too full of emotion. She tried to struggle free but he would not let go, and then his mother appeared in the doorway.

'Melissa.' He spoke to her softly but urgently, his frown momentarily fading, nothing but kindness in his eyes. 'Melissa, I want you to go back to your room and wait for me. Everything will be all right, I promise. But I must speak to my mother first. You will do that?'

What other choice had she? He would stop her before she got to the front door. She nodded miserably.

'Good.' He pressed a kiss to her brow and ushered her back into the bedroom, and his face changed dramatically as he turned to his mother. His brow furrowed even more deeply, his eyes darkened. He was clearly extremely angry. What an effort it must have been to hold himself in check.

She closed the door, not wanting to see or hear what was going on, and sat on the edge of the bed. He had heard what his mother had said and was rightly annoyed with her, but Melissa was glad she had learned the truth.

Benedict had used her, he had used her as a shield against Felicity. And God, how it hurt.

To think there had been moments when she almost believed that he was serious! And yet all he had been trying to do was make sure she would not let him down by confessing their engagement wasn't for real. How gullible she had been!

But his mother knew the truth now whether he wanted her to or not, and she guessed it wouldn't be long before Felicity was acquainted with the facts, too.

Melissa's throat felt as though it was closing up on her. She swallowed with difficulty and tears pricked the back of her eyes. He had been so thoughtful and caring and loving these last few days, she had really thought—no, she had hoped, that he was falling in love with her, that she had been wrong to mistrust him, that he wanted more from her than a love affair.

Now she knew better. He could talk to her and console her and tell her to forget and ignore what his mother had said, but it would make no difference. He didn't love Felicity, but neither did he love her. Perhaps he was incapable of loving. There must be something wrong, that he had reached the age of thirty-five without getting married.

And if things really were all over between him and this girl then he should make her see it, and put an end to her nonsense. Then there would be no need for such ridiculous games. Surely he must have realised how his mother would treat her? Patricia Cameron had made no secret at all of her preference for the other girl.

It seemed an age before he finally came to her. His eyes were troubled; he looked sad, but no longer angry. 'Melissa, I'm sorry. I had no idea what my mother was up to.' He took her hands and held them in his big warm ones.

It would have felt comforting, except that she wouldn't let it. Inside, deep down inside, she was fighting him, fighting herself, the awareness, the love, the need. How she needed him. He had stolen up on her unawares. She had wanted no one, she had fought against him, for weeks she had fought, and in the end there had been no point in fighting any longer. She loved him. And she guessed she always would. She just hoped he had not heard her tell his mother.

'You can't answer for her,' she said quietly. 'She did what she felt she had to.'

'What she said is unforgivable.'

Melissa shrugged. 'It doesn't matter. I shan't ever see her again. I've served my purpose.'

A muscle jerked in his jaw. 'You think that?'

'What else am I supposed to think? Both your mother and Felicity made a point of telling me that she was in love with you, and that in time you would come to your senses. You say that's not possible, and I believe you, but there's no future for us together, either.' It was clear now that he had not heard her declaration of love. What a relief.

'Felicity spoke to you as well?' The anger was back in his eyes.

She nodded.

'Why didn't you tell me?'

'There seemed no point. It wasn't as if we were truly engaged. I hope you don't marry her, though, Benedict.'

'I made that quite clear tonight,' he said tersely. 'I don't think she'll bother me again. Felicity was an unfortunate mistake.'

'Have you told your mother that there's no chance of you and Felicity ever getting together again?'

'Repeatedly,' he grimaced. 'I also told her she owes you an apology.'

'No!' Melissa shook her head emphatically. 'That's not necessary. I'd rather I didn't see her again. Can't we leave now?'

'We could, but I think a few hours' sleep would do us both good.' He looked at his watch. 'It is after two.'

'I suppose you're right.' But Melissa was sure she would not sleep. Too much had happened.

She did sleep, however, and she woke the next morning feeling better, though not much. She did not want to see Mrs Cameron; she did not want to be forced to accept her apology. She wanted to get away now, before anyone else was up.

She splashed her face with water and pulled on a pair of white jeans and a white knitted top and then went and tapped on Benedict's door.

It was opened immediately. He wore his trousers but nothing else. He was freshly shaven and he smelled good and Melissa felt the familiar thrill ride through her. 'I'm ready to go,' she whispered huskily.

'Are you positive you don't want to see my mother?' he asked, beckoning her inside. 'She will apologise, I assure you.

'I'd rather not.'

He nodded, as though understanding, and she stood and watched as he pulled on his socks and shoes. She had an insane urge to go and stand close to him, to slide her arms around that silken hard body, to feel him and hold him and beg him to never let her go. But how impossible that was.

She moved to the window as he buttoned his shirt, looking down at the tables and chairs on the patio, the empty glasses and dirty plates, all left to be dealt with this morning. Had it been her party, thought Melissa, she would have cleared everything last night. There would have been nothing to do this morning. Patricia Cameron, though, had had other things on her mind.

She swung around. 'Are you ready?' Thinking about his mother increased her despondency and she was eager to get away.

He pushed the last of his things into his suitcase and snapped the locks. 'I am now.'

They collected her case and in the hall met his mother. She was wearing a long quilted dressing-gown and her face was bare of make-up and she looked her age. 'I believe I owe you an apology,' she said stiltedly to Melissa. It was obviously an effort to get the words out.

Melissa lifted her shoulders. 'It doesn't matter.'

'Oh, but it does,' said Benedict fiercely.

'I shouldn't have spoken to you like I did,' said the woman. 'I'm sorry.'

Like hell she was, thought Melissa. All she was doing was attempting to appease her son. She inclined her head. 'Thank you, and thank you for your hospitality.'

'And now we are going,' said Benedict. 'Say goodbye to David for us.'

'Won't you stop and have breakfast?' Patricia Cameron looked hurt.

He shook his head, his mouth grim. 'I'm afraid that's

impossible.'

They went out to the hired car and Melissa wished it were Benedict's own so that they could go straight to Vivienne's. It was going to be a long and tiring journey before they finally got to Oxford.

For the first quarter of an hour they drove in silence and then Melissa spoke. 'I hope I haven't caused too much unpleasantness between you and your mother.' She had actually felt sorry for Mrs Cameron in those last moments of parting. The woman had looked anguished. Instead of getting rid of her son's new girlfriend, she had caused a rift between him and herself.

'Nothing that won't mend eventually,' he said firmly. 'It's not the first time we haven't seen eye to eye.'

'I felt sorry for her this morning,' said Melissa.

'She has a thick skin,' he said. 'I shouldn't worry too much. The next time I see her she'll have forgotten all about it. Besides, she has to accept the fact that I shall never marry Felicity.'

When they reached London and returned the car Benedict said, 'Do you still want to go home, or shall be book into a hotel for the night? We have a lot of talking to do.'

'About what?' asked Melissa crisply. 'The way you tried to use me? It was despicable. I don't think I shall ever forgive you.' If she had not loved him so much she might have found it amusing, but at this moment all she could feel was hurt.

'Is it any use saying I'm sorry?' He looked desperately sad, but she hardened her heart.

'No. You knew how much I'd been hurt in the past. You knew I was seeking sanctuary when I went to Vivienne's. How you could do this to me?'

He looked at her long and hard and every nerve in her body responded to him, and she ached to be taken into his arms. What madness it all was. He had used her and yet still she loved him, and wanted him, and needed him. Why, oh why, did he not love her? Why had it happened to her all over again? Was there no man in this world who would love her as she wanted to be loved, and whom she could love in return?

'It was never my intention to hurt you, Melly.'

'Perhaps not,' she said in a quiet little voice. 'I don't want to discuss it any more. All I want to do is go home and be allowed to lead my life the way I want to. Without interference from you or Vivienne or anyone else.'

He hailed a taxi, and then they had to wait an hour for a train. A silent, miserable hour. They didn't speak on the journey, either, each wrapped in their own unhappy thoughts.

This was the end, thought Melissa. There was no possible future between them now. All her hopes and dreams had been for nothing—and she could not even discuss it with Vivienne.

It was almost one when they got home. Melissa would have felt mean letting him go up to his empty flat without offering him a meal. 'I'll cook us some lunch, if you like,' she said, knowing full well that even the tiniest mouthful would choke her.

Mentally she crossed her fingers that he would refuse, but he smiled and looked pleased. 'That would be nice.'

She cooked while he watched. The omelette went flat, but Benedict swore it was the best he had ever tasted. Afterwards he sent her out into the garden while he washed up, and when he joined her she said, 'Do you think we should go to the office?'

'I'd rather stay here and make you fall in love with me.'

Melissa swallowed hard, unconsciously twisting his ring on her finger. 'There's no more need for pretence, Benedict. I suppose I should give you this back.'

'I love you,' he said.

He spoke so softly, she almost did not hear him. Her eyes widened and her heart galloped. 'What did you say?'

'Something I had no intention of admitting until I was sure how you felt. But I can't wait for ever.'

'Benedict?' Her voice was a breathless whisper.

'It's true,' he said. 'Have I shocked you?'

Melissa closed her eyes and let out an unsteady breath. Benedict loved her! It was an impossible dream come true.

She looked at him and saw for the first time his love for her shining in his eyes. She felt suddenly special and beautiful and wanted, and excited and sexy, and very very feminine, and she knew that she would love him for the rest of her life, and that nothing would ever go wrong.

'Shock is too mild a word,' she said. 'Oh, Benedict, Benedict.' She felt close to tears. 'I love you, too.'

For an instant he looked completely taken aback. He just looked at her with a frown on his forehead and wonder in his eyes. Then, when he realised she was serious, his eyes softened and he smiled as he took her hand across the table. 'Thank God, Melly. Thank God. I never thought the day would come.'

'And I never thought you felt like that about me,' she whispered painfully. 'I thought you just—wanted me.'

'Hell, that as well,' he groaned. 'Desperately,

agonisingly. But first and foremost I want your trust in me.'

Their eyes met and held, for years and years, and then she said quietly, 'You have it, Benedict, for all time.'

'My Melly.' He got up and came round the table, and she rose. His arms went about her, and he held her for a long, long time. Then she lifted her chin and there were tears in her eyes. He kissed them away and his mouth sought hers and they drank each other's love as though they had found water in the desert.

At length they broke apart. He looked at her and shook his head, and smiled, and made her feel as though she were melting. 'We almost never made it.'

Ruefully she nodded. 'It was all my fault. I let what happened with Tim ruin me for any other man.'

'Thank God I'm tenacious,' he grinned. 'It's been a long, uphill struggle. That day you said you had no intention of falling in love again I despaired of this moment ever happening. Hence the *fait accompli* at my mother's. It was a last hope. And what a failure. I've never cried in my life, Melly, but I wanted to last night. Everything had fallen to pieces. My mother had ruined the whole damned thing.'

'Do you think she'll learn to like me, in time?'

'I'm sure she will,' he said. 'How can she not love you? You're the girl I've been waiting for all my life.'

And with confidence like that, how could Melissa doubt that their future together would be good?

'Do you remember that night I had the nightmare,' she said, when they broke off from a kiss that had lasted for ever, 'and you held me against your chest and I cried? And then I laughed and you thought I was hysterical and you slapped me?'

He looked down at her tenderly. 'Could I ever forget? Every minute I've spent with you is embedded in my memory.'

'Well,' she said with a shy smile, 'I think I ought to tell you that that was the moment my idea for the diamond commercial was born.'

His brows rose questioningly.

'My tears on your chest looked like diamonds. I wanted to tell you then but I was afraid. You didn't seem to take too kindly to the idea of my coming up with suggestions.'

'Hell, Melly,' he groaned. 'I didn't want to admit that you were clever. All the time I wanted to think the worst of you. But I couldn't. Even in those dreadful clothes you were the sexiest creature on earth, and the most efficient. Is it any wonder I fell in love with you?'

Melissa reached up and kissed him. 'And when they were actually filming the commercial and you accused me of living every moment of the scene——'

'Because I thought you were thinking of Tim, or the model, or even Clifford, dammit.' He looked angry for a second.

She smiled and touched her fingers to his face. 'I was thinking about you. I was imagining us lying together. It should be you in that advert, Benedict. In my mind it always will be.'

He groaned again and held her tightly, and she felt a tremor run through him. 'Exactly when did you realise you'd fallen in love with me—and why the hell didn't you tell me?'

'I was strongly attracted right from the beginning,' she admitted. 'I think you knew that. But it wasn't until we were in Paris and you were so angry about those flowers Clifford sent me, and then he came and you saw me in his arms, that I knew. I'd half suspected if before, but I wouldn't admit it, even to myself. I didn't want to fall in love.'

'But you couldn't help yourself?'

She nodded.

'Neither could I. I guess we were meant for each other. One thing I promise you, Melly, I'll never, ever let you down.'

'I know,' she whispered. She felt safe and secure for the first time since Tim had jilted her. 'I wonder what Vivienne will say?'

'That it's about time,' he laughed. 'She thought I was crazy for not telling you how I felt.'

'She thought I was, too,' admitted Melissa. 'She told me she suspected you loved me, but I wouldn't believe her.'

'Suspected be damned! She knew. And hell, was I jealous of Clifford.'

'He really did help me,' said Melissa. 'And I still want to be friends with him, even after we're married.'

'You're sure there was nothing between you?' he asked fiercely.

'He loved me,' she admitted sadly, 'but I didn't love him, and he never did anything other than kiss me. He's such a patient man. He was waiting for me to get over Tim. It really hurt him when he discovered I loved you, but even so he put my happiness first. He's in America now. Did you know? He went so that I would stop seeing him and hopefully get together with you.'

Benedict's eyes narrowed. 'He did that for you?'

She nodded.

'Then he's a better man than me. I could never have left you.' He kissed her again and time was forgotten. Melissa had no doubt now that he loved her, and her future looked happy and secure. No matter what happened, because life was never one smooth passage—she had found that out already—he would be beside her, and they would weather the storms together.

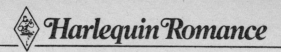
Harlequin Romance

Coming Next Month

Take 4 best-selling love stories FREE
Plus get a FREE surprise gift!

Taylor House

by Leigh Anne Williams

Enter the lives of the Taylor women of Greensdale, Massachusetts, a town where tradition and family mean so much. A story of family, home and love in a New England village.

Don't miss the Taylor House trilogy, starting next month in Harlequin American Romance with #265 *Katherine's Dream*, in October 1988, and followed by #269 *Lydia's Hope* and #273 *Clarissa's Wish* in November and December of 1988.

One house . . . two sisters . . . three generations

If *YOU* enjoyed this book,
your daughter may enjoy

Keepsake

Romances from

CROSSWINDS

Keepsake is a series of tender, funny, down-to-earth romances for younger teens.

The simple boy-meets-girl romances have lively and believable characters, lots of action and romantic situations with which teens can identify.

Available now wherever books are sold.